# Crossroads of Faith

Modern-Day stories
based on
biblical parables
and events

## *Bobby J Watson*

The Testing          Like A Fox

The Unexpected

Rooted          The Escape

# Table of Contents

This book is dedicated to
the memory of my grandmother
Annie Springs Orr, one of the
truly good people this world has known.

# Introduction

The following stories are all inspired by biblical parables and events. Some are modern day retellings of the original passages, while others were simply inspired by them. If you are a regular bible reader or have a church background, you may recognize the source of each story as you read it.

Even if you're not that familiar with the passages, you will find the stories themselves to be both entertaining and compelling. They contain trials of faith and life that we all may experience at one time or another. Each tale presents biblical wisdom in how to deal with these trials and challenges us to be the best version of ourselves.

For a little fun as you read, try to identify the original parable or event upon which the story is based. You may find some to be pretty easy to identify and others a bit more challenging. But don't worry. If you aren't sure about the source or simply have no clue, that's okay. The epilogue at the end of each tale will reveal the passages behind the story.

Now, have fun and happy reading!

# The Unexpected

by
*Bobby J Watson*

*Character is doing the right thing when nobody is looking.*

**- J.C. Watts**

# Chapter One

Bryan Harris had travelled from his office in the city of Garrison to the town of Kingsville which was about thirty miles away. It was a pretty quick drive on the Interstate Highway that connected the two locales, but not a particularly scenic drive. Once in Kingsville he had met with a real estate agent and looked at several properties. He had no interest in moving to the town. He actually considered living in Kingsville a step down on the ladder of success, but he was thinking about buying some rental property to add to his inventory of houses.

Bryan currently had six houses in the Garrison area that he rented. He had bought them over the last couple of years and they had yielded not only additional income but had grown in value. Kingsville was a town of mostly lower to middle income blue collar workers and seemed like a ripe area to grow his business. So he had spent the day looking at several homes and had settled on two that seemed like a good start. The owners of both had recently been laid off their jobs and were in some financial distress, but Bryan didn't feel right taking advantage of their situation. As much as he liked making money and finding good deals, he considered himself a Christian and felt he needed to offer them what he thought the homes were worth and not what he thought they would settle for.

The first home was a three bedroom frame house that was well constructed and in good condition. It had one and a half baths and a one-car garage. When he offered the couple who owned it the price they had listed, they seemed somewhat shocked and immediately accepted his offer. Bryan felt like it was a fair value and he would quickly turn it to profit.

The second home was a four bedroom brick with two baths and a two-car garage consisting of a little over 2300 square feet. However it was in bad need of both interior and exterior painting and also needed new carpet and drapes. He offered ten thousand less than the owners had asked because he knew it would take that much to get it into shape to rent. They hesitated initially but then consented to the deal, knowing they would not get a better offer.

He then conferred with the agent, who promised to arrange closing dates as soon as possible with the title company. Since Bryan would be paying cash they should be able to close within a couple of weeks. He shook hands with the agent and prepared to make the drive back to Garrison. While it was faster to take the interstate back home, he decided instead that he would take an alternate route that wound through the nearby hills and was much more scenic. He didn't get to Kingsville that often and he actually enjoyed driving the winding road through the hills. There was something magical and very comforting about it, and he had no reason to rush home today.

He called his wife, Andrea, and told her about the deals he had made. Andrea wasn't that interested in the purchase process, but she usually got involved in any upgrades such as painting or carpeting for the rental properties. Once the sales were closed she would go with him to inspect the houses and help decide on colors and other details. He then spoke to his five year old son, Aaron, and told him that he would be home in time to tell him goodnight. Bryan loved his family. They were the main catalyst that motivated him to be the best provider he could be. When they had married, he had no real interest in church but Andrea was a regular attender and so he sometimes would go with her. He found himself getting more and more interested in the gospel with each visit and after about six months of attending, he had made the choice to accept Christ and get baptized. They had attended regularly as a family ever since. He was no bible thumper or leader of any kind, but he did try to read devotionals daily and live the best life for God that he could.

As he drove out of Kingsville he noticed that it was now about 5:30 and he decided to stop for something to eat. Finding a diner on the outskirts of town he stopped there and went inside. Looking at the menu he decided it was a good time to have breakfast for dinner. Actually for Bryan almost any day was a good one to have breakfast for dinner. So he ordered two eggs over medium, pancakes and corned beef hash. He washed it down with two cups of black coffee. Paying the cashier, he visited their restroom, which was surprisingly clean, and then returned to his car.

It was now a few minutes past 6:00 but there was still about thirty minutes of daylight so he could enjoy most of the drive before it turned dark. He opened the sunroof on his SUV to let in the fresh air and enhance his view of the surroundings. Navigating the first sharp curve about two miles down the road from the diner, he felt a calm flow over him. He wasn't sure why he found this drive so comforting but he always did. Part of the charm was of course the sheer beauty of the hillsides, but another feature was the sense of being alone. Most people nowadays took the interstate and very few chose this path, especially with night coming so soon. He would be surprised if he saw more than half a dozen other vehicles on his route.

He had no inkling that this particular drive would hold no comfort at all and in fact would change his life in ways that he could not even imagine.

# Chapter Two

He was nearly halfway down the lonely road when he rounded yet another curve and heard a loud popping noise, almost like an explosion. The car lunged to his right and he fought to maintain control as he pressed hard on the brakes. The car continued to fight against him but he managed to keep it on the road and as it finally slowed down to a crawl he heard the unhappy but familiar sound of flat rubber hitting the road. The right rear tire had blown and was now coming to pieces as he came to a stop.

His first instinct was to call roadside assistance. He had a plan through his cell phone provider and this was the perfect time to use it. He had on a suit with a white shirt and necktie and wasn't thrilled with the idea of getting them dirty and sweaty changing a tire. He started to dial the number on his iPhone but noticed that he had no service. That was one disadvantage of this route that he hadn't considered or even thought would be an issue, but now he took off his suit coat and necktie and got the jack out of the rear of the SUV. He had changed flats before, but he had never changed one on this car, and it took him a minute to locate the tool and figure out how this particular jack worked. He then got on his knees and looked underneath the vehicle, finding a spot that would provide good support to lift the car.

First he loosened the lug nuts and started jacking the car up, inch by inch until it cleared the ground by about six inches. He pulled the old tire off and started to toss it aside as it was beyond fixing, but then he thought "why trash the roadside with it" and leaned it against the car. The spare was a full sized tire, which surprised him a little bit, and he put it in place and tightened the lug nuts. After lowering the car to the ground, he tightened the lug nuts a final time. He would have the tire store check for tightness when he bought a new tire tomorrow. He put the jack back in place and tossed the old tire in back of the SUV.

Wiping the grime off his hands as best he could, he prepared to continue on home. He couldn't wait to get there now.

Just as he closed the tailgate he was surprised to see another car, actually a four-door pickup truck, pull up behind him. Three strong looking young men got out and the driver asked, "Sir, are you okay? Did you have some trouble?"

Bryan couldn't help but laugh a little as he replied, "I'm fine. Just had a flat tire. I could have used you guys a few minutes ago." Coming closer the driver agreed, "Yes sir it looks like we were a few minutes late, or maybe we were just in time." Now the three men were on each side and in front of him and the car was behind him. Bryan realized he was trapped unless they moved. "I appreciate you guys stopping, but it's all good now and I need to get on home."

These words had barely escaped his lips when he felt the first blow to his kidney. Then the guy on the other side punched him and the driver who was in front rammed his fist into Bryan's solar plexus knocking the air out of him and making him go to his knees. All three continued to pummel him with blow after blow and then kicked him mercilessly when he crumbled prone on the ground. He went blank and only had a vague, fuzzy memory of hearing the sadistic laughter of the trio and then the pickup and his SUV driving off down the road, leaving him alone and helpless.

When he fully came to again it was dark. He no idea what time it was and his iPhone had been in the car so he couldn't check the time with it either. No matter, he slowly got to his feet and as he did sharp pain hit him from every direction and dizziness made it hard to remain standing. He reached for his head and found a large bump on the crown of his skull. When he pulled his hand back it was damp and dark with blood. He wasn't a doctor and didn't know that much about anatomy but from what he remembered he thought the pain on his back and side was around his kidneys and spleen. He had never experienced pain like this before, not even when hit by a linebacker in his high school football days.

He knew that he couldn't stay there and also knew there was little chance of a passerby coming to his rescue. So he started slowly walking in the direction in which he had been driving. Both towns were about the same distance from him but Garrison would have more traffic as he got closer and also better medical facilities. Besides it was home.

He had walked maybe two hundred yards when his legs would move no more. He sunk down to a sitting position and hung his head down. The pain was too much and he had no stamina. He would rest and then go again, but he knew he would never make it like this. He looked up to the heavens. The stars were now out and a half-moon was starting to rise. He lifted his voice. "Father God in heaven, hear my plea Lord. I need your help. I can't do this on my own. Please send someone, Lord. Send someone to help me. Lord, I love you and I love Andrea and Aaron. Please help me get home to them."

As he finished the prayer Bryan grew quiet and listened. In the distance he heard the hoot of an owl followed by crickets chirping. And then silence. He had hoped to hear the sound of a motor coming his way but no, just silence. A tear rolled down his cheek as he struggled to get on his feet. How long would he be able to walk this time?

# Chapter Three

Clifton Cosgrove lived on the east side of Garrison in an upscale community of large homes called The Sanctuary. It was marked by well-manicured lawns and season appropriate flower beds. Homes had two and three car garages and the contents tended to be BMW's, Lincoln Aviators, Mercedes and other luxury vehicles. The homeowners were typically doctors, lawyers, and company executives at the crescent of their careers. Clifton Cosgrove didn't quite fit these categories but his bank account certainly qualified him for membership in the community. Clifton was actually an evangelist.

Years ago when he had first graduated from seminary he had taken a position as assistant pastor of a church comprised mostly of middle income professionals and blue collar workers. He liked the job at first but soon tired of the routine. He also found himself disagreeing with the sermon topics chosen by the senior pastor. The pastor's sermons were usually geared toward helping the congregants grow spiritually and offered ideas about how to serve the Lord better. He always included an altar call but evangelism seemed to always take a secondary role, at least in Clifton's opinion.

After an eighteen month stint at the church, he accepted an offer to be the lead pastor at a small church in a nearby town. Now he could preach what he chose and focus on the topics he felt were important. His fiery brand of sermonizing was warmly greeted by the members at first, but after a few months some of the deacons and other influential members suggested that sermons to help the members grow would be beneficial. Clifton tried to adjust his approach but this just was not him and he found it difficult to stay on that track. He was also getting tired of the routine, just as he had at the previous church. Seeing the same people week after week, hearing the same complaints and sob stories week after week, visiting the sick in hospitals every week grew old and after a year he decided to leave the church. He just needed to find something that fit his personality better. Also, something that paid better would help. He now had a wife and a child on the way and he wanted them to have the best.

One day after he resigned and was sitting at home flipping through television channels, he stumbled upon a Christian broadcasting channel and watched an evangelist who had the crowd shouting for joy and raising their hands to the Lord. He of course had seen this many times in his life, but the thought of him doing it had never occurred to him. Now he imagined what it would be like to preach to large crowds of new faces every night and feel the excitement in the air.

The next day he started working on a plan to present himself as an evangelist who would go from church to church and preach revivals. He could see himself reinvigorating dying congregations and winning the lost to Christ. Preaching two or three days in a row and then moving to another church and another audience appealed to him. This was what he was meant to do.

It started out slowly. He managed to secure engagements in a few small country churches, and churches in small towns that were struggling. His wife would often travel with him. She had a lovely voice and sang the old gospel songs that appealed to these small congregations. He learned to build his message from a whisper to a final crescendo that had people standing and shouting, whooping, raising their hands and praising the Lord. The atmosphere he created was almost like an old-time tent revival.

He developed a skill for mentioning something about his growing family and telling the audience how a road pastor struggles to make ends meet into each sermon. He was never too overt, but subtly brought this out every night. At the end of each service a love offering was taken and mentioning these struggles helped fill the collection plates to overflowing every time. He also made a point to gently pump each pastor to mention him and the success they had at pastors' meetings and other events. Word of mouth was the best way to grow his number of engagements.

Eventually, he began to receive invitations to preach in larger churches in bigger cities. He didn't tone down his enthusiasm for these crowds but he did learn to change his subject matter to be more relevant to their needs. He still preached the need for God and for them to make a commitment and avoid the eternal damnation that awaited the unbeliever, but he also used the carrot as well as the stick. He talked more about how God blessed the believer with success in their careers and even riches beyond what they could imagine. If you had enough faith then God would bless you with whatever you asked. Some called it the prosperity gospel and maybe it was, but hadn't God in fact promised to hear and answer the prayers of the righteous? To give them what they asked? Of course this worked for him as well and those love offerings grew substantially in the larger venues, so that today he and his wife and three kids could live in The Sanctuary.

The church in Kingsville had asked him several times to fit them into his schedule. Honestly, that church was much smaller than the ones he now appeared in but it was close to home and he finally had agreed to a three night revival there, mostly just so he could spend a few additional days at home with his family. Nice as the current situation was, he sometimes grew tired of the constant travel and craved time at home.

So this afternoon he got into his new Cadillac Escalade and drove to Kingsville. His wife stayed home with the children so it was just him tonight. He would go and preach and hopefully be home before the kids' bedtime.

# Chapter Four

The evening started with a meeting with the Kingsville church pastor where they discussed the pastor's hopes and expectations for the revival. He shared some of the problems the church was experiencing. As was nearly always the case the finances were not what they should be and he hoped the revival would increase attendance and hence the weekly offerings. He also shared his concern for the community and the lack of enthusiasm that so many young people had for church these days. He hoped that the messages, and especially those on the final night which was youth night, could stir young people to be emboldened and to share with their friends and invite them to church. Of course there were also the inevitable personal issues that all churches seemed to have. Some of the lay leadership had expressed disappointment and disagreement about specific issues and methods the pastor utilized. He hoped they could come out of the revival more unified as a body of believers.

Clifton could have recited most of these concerns before even arriving at the pastor's study. He had heard them at almost every church where he preached. He of course sympathized and agreed with the pastor and they prayed that the revival would be a great success and make progress with these items. They then shared a light meal consisting of cheese and crackers with some assorted fruit slices. They had sweet tea along with this. Clifton liked to have a light meal prior to the service but nothing too heavy. Once he was home he would have a heftier meal that fully assuaged his appetite.

The service itself seemed to go well. He was in good form as he preached the wages of sin and the benefits of accepting God into one's life. The congregation grew more animated as he went along and by the end several were standing and waving their hands to the heavens and yelling "amens" and "hallelujahs". The offering was more than he expected from this relatively small church.

At the end of the service they sang the old hymns "When We All Get to Heaven" and "I Surrender All" as he and the pastor urged anyone who had made a decision to change their life, accept Christ and be baptized to come forward. Three young women in their twenties had come to the altar, as well as two teenage boys. Finally a little guy about nine or ten years old had come down, trembling with fear and with tears in his eyes. He told Clifton that he didn't want to go to hell. He wanted to get on the path to heaven. Clifton praised his decision and shared it with the congregation who clapped enthusiastically. He had preached a fiery hell and damnation sermon and thought to himself that it was better to scare the little boy into heaven rather than leave him on the road to hell.

As the service ended and people started to go to their homes, he hoped to make a quick exit but there are always those who want to shake your hand and tell you their stories so he patiently waded through that process. By the time he was getting into his car it was nearly 8:00 and already dark. He had been surprised by how far the church was from the interstate and so he decided maybe it would be faster to take the old highway instead. It was only a block away from the building and should have very little traffic.

As he drove through the hilly countryside he thought about tomorrow night's service. He hoped he could convince his wife to come and sing a couple of songs. People always loved her singing and responded well to the songs she chose. The two youngest kids, girls, could stay in the church nursery. The oldest, his son, was only seven but he could sit with his mom after she had sang. He got few opportunities for his son to watch him work and welcomed the opportunity. Even though he was still very young, Clifton envisioned a time when they would be a father and son duo preaching the gospel across the land. Perhaps that was just ego but it was something he often thought about and imagined.

He rounded a particularly sharp curve and his headlights shone on the image of a man up in the distance. As he approached the man he slowed his Cadillac down and studied him. He was obviously disheveled and seemed to stagger as he turned toward the approaching car and lifted his hand, signaling that he needed a ride. Clifton thought to himself *"Oh, dear. That man is probably homeless and it looks like he might even be drunk. A bum. Can you imagine what people would say if I showed up in town with him in my car?"* He eased by the man, trying not to make eye contact and then picked up speed as he passed him. He couldn't get away quickly enough.

Bryan had heard the car coming from some distance behind him. The engine groaned and the transmission strained to cope with the hilly terrain. He hoped that this would be a friendly soul who would give him a ride to town. He thought it would be obvious to anyone that he had encountered trouble and needed a little help. His heart surged as the car approached and seemed to slow down. He turned, now that it was in sight, and lifted his hand in the universal sign for hitchhiking. The car slowed a little more and he began to feel sure it was going to stop. This was the answer to his earlier prayer.

But then his anticipation weakened when the car never came to a complete stop. The driver was a man about his own age in a nice suit and tie just as he had earlier been wearing. The man looked at him initially but then seemed to turn his eyes back to the road. The car began to pick up speed then and soon was around the next curve and out of sight.

Bryan couldn't believe it. He dropped to his knees and it seemed that all hope just left him. He sat there for probably ten minutes but then he thought about Andrea and Aaron and resolved to stand up and continue his journey. He thought to himself that if God could send one car, he could send another. He just hoped it would come soon. His final thought was that the SUV seemed familiar, that it looked like one he had seen near in his neighborhood in Garrison, The Sanctuary.

# Chapter Five

Herbert Clawson was an independent insurance agent. His agency consisted of himself and an assistant named Brenda who had been with him for several years. The agency handled all types of insurance including auto, homeowners, life and business insurance. He had been working the area around Garrison for nearly twenty years and while there were bigger agencies, he had managed to grow his into a successful venture with a loyal set of clients. Most of the business was in home and auto, but he also sold a number of life insurance policies. He had long ago learned to couple the need for homeowners insurance with a life policy on the principal bread winner so that if tragedy struck, the rest of the family would be assured they could stay in the home.

Over the past couple of years however, he had delved more into commercial insurance and focused on growing that part of his portfolio of clients. That's what had taken him to Kingsville today. He had met with the owner of a small auto repair shop and sold him a complete policy. He had started by explaining how garage liability insurance would cover the business if a mistake or omission was made in a repair and it resulted in damage to a customer's vehicle. He was lucky in a way because the previous month that very thing had happened when a worker failed to secure the oil pan cap and the engine had gone out on a customer's car. The owner, a man of about fifty named Marvin Callicut, couldn't deny the mistake and had to replace the engine at his own expense. Herbert, or Herb as friends called him, added this, "And what if the blown engine had caused the owner to crash the car or even hit another car? You might have been out of business with the liability that would bring." The owner thought about that and agreed that he was probably lucky he only had to replace the engine.

Once this part of the sale was secured, Herb went on to explain loss of use coverage to the owner.  In case of fire or some other disaster, how would he replace the temporary loss of revenue until he was back in business?  How would he continue to pay and retain his mechanics and other employees?  Again Callicut reluctantly agreed that this would be devastating and he should have protection against something like that.

Lastly Herb went for the two final issues.  The man had insurance on his building, but why hadn't that insurance agent pointed out these additional coverage requirements?  Herb knew the agent and knew he probably had mentioned these and the owner had rejected it at the time, but that was a few years ago and Callicut had undoubtedly forgotten.  Herb reviewed that current policy and pointed out that it expired next month so they could go ahead and agree to a new policy today and make it effective on that date.  Again the owner agreed.

The final issue was one he thought might be pushing things too far, but he presented it anyhow.  Key-man life insurance would provide his wife or any future partner the means and the funds to carry on the business in the unlikely event that Marvin became deceased.  You never said the word "died" when selling life insurance.  You always opted for "deceased" instead.  It sounded so much nicer.  Mr. Callicut explained that he had recently remarried and two teenage sons came with the new spouse.  He hoped someday one of them would become involved in the business and he certainly wanted to protect them and give them a fair chance to continue the business if something happened to him.  So yes, he might as well do for the key-man coverage also.  He was in good health and didn't smoke so it should be relatively inexpensive.

Herb was feeling elated and invited the auto shop owner to dine with him before he started the drive back to Garrison.  "Marv, can I call you Marv?"  After receiving a nod of approval he continued.  "Marv why don't you lead and I'll follow.  You know the town and restaurants here better than I do, so just lead

*19*

me to your favorite one." Marv's favorite turned out to be a little diner on the outskirts of Kingsville. He ordered a chicken fried steak and mashed potatoes, while Herb opted for two grilled pork chops and steamed veggies. They chatted about their businesses for a while and then about their families. Marv was a widower and had three grown children from his first marriage and two grandsons, but they had all moved away from the area and he seldom saw them except on holidays. His new spouse had the two teenagers and Marv thought he had developed a good rapport with them. Herb shared that he had been married to JoAnn for twelve years and they had two children who were in elementary school. They both chose the apple cobbler ala mode for dessert and then each headed to their own homes.

Herb noted that the diner was on the old highway. Normally he would have returned home on the interstate but that would require backtracking so he decided to stay on the old road. He climbed into his Ford Edge SUV and started the drive home. It was a winding road and he hadn't taken it in years, but he remembered that it was a scenic route and he sort of wished it wasn't getting dark so quickly. He would have enjoyed the scenery.

As he drove he remembered that his wife was planning to take their son and some other kids to soccer practice tomorrow. The parents rotated who would pick up the kids from school, go to practice, and then deliver them home and it was her turn. That meant she would need the Edge tomorrow and he would drive his Ford F150 pickup truck to the office.

Herb was on the deacon board at church and in fact was the chairman this year. He had served for about eight years now and was one of the senior members of the board. They had a meeting scheduled for tomorrow night to discuss the pastor's ideas about augmenting Sunday School with Life Groups. He had heard other churches starting similar groups with some success, but some of the board members feared it would cause a decline in adult Sunday School attendance. Herb himself didn't see the need for these new groups but he was open to hearing what the pastor had to say.

These things were floating through his mind when he rounded a curve and saw something on the side of road. At first he didn't recognize the object, but as he drew closer he saw that it was a man sitting on the roadside. The shock of seeing someone so expectantly made him hit his brakes unnecessarily, almost coming to a complete stop. *What in the world is someone doing out here,* he thought to himself. The man, whoever he was, seemed just as shocked as Herb.

They had both just encountered something that neither expected.

# Chapter Six

The man seemed to struggle to rise to his feet and hold out his hand to signal a ride. Herb slowed down and the first thing he noted was that the man seemed absolutely filthy. Then he noticed what might have been blood on the man's shirt. At first Herb was touched and felt sorry for the fellow, but then as he considered the image more, he thought to himself *"Another homeless guy, these people really need to take care of themselves. He's probably on drugs or something."* Then he whispered out loud to himself "Can you imagine how the car would smell if I picked him up? JoAnn would kill me."

With that thought lingering in his mind, he accelerated and continued home.

Bryan had walked again just as far as he could, this time about forty yards. Each trek seemed to be shorter than the previous one. Sinking to the ground, he had never felt so hopeless and alone in his whole life. His mind drifted to the three young guys who had stolen his SUV. His first thought was pure hate and he wished he could kill them. Then he wondered what they would do with the vehicle. Were there chop shops in Garrison? Would they take it somewhere else? Would they just take it for a joy ride and abandon it? He had heard of young people doing things like that. His thought then went back to them and this time he felt kind of sorry for them rather than hateful. What kind of lives had they lived? How had they been raised to end up doing something like this? He then thought of Aaron and promised himself that Aaron would grow up knowing he was loved and not wanting to do harm to anyone, and he would respect people's property like it was his own.

Then he started feeling very weak and sleep or something like it seemed to overcome him. Was he going to sleep or losing consciousness? He wasn't sure but whatever it was, he seemed unable to stop it. Then in the far distance he heard the sound of an engine again. Was it real or his imagination? Maybe the first man had turned back to help him. No, this was from the direction of Kingsville. It must be another car.

Just then a large Ford Edge rounded the curve to his left and slammed on its brakes. The shrieking sound scared Bryan awake and he thought the car was about to hit him! But then it stopped and the driver looked intently at him. Bryan struggled to his feet with an effort accompanied by great pain and held up his hand. *I just need a ride, Mister. I've been beat up.* The look on the driver's face seemed to magically turn from one of sympathy and curiosity to one of scorn. Like the first driver he then turned back into the road and moved past Bryan. This time the man left so quickly that he spun his tires and slung gravel all over the side of the road. Bryan was lucky that none of it hit him.

Bryan slumped to the road again and this time he cried openly with tears streaming down his face. *Lord, why is this happening to me? Why won't you hear my prayer and help me?* He thought back into his past and wondered if he had done something to deserve this. Sure, he wasn't perfect but he didn't know of anything that warranted this degree of punishment. His thoughts once again went to Andrea and Aaron. He had to survive somehow. They were all that was important now and he had to get back to them no matter what it took. In his mind his resolve grew, but his body was still weak and racked with pain like he had never known.

He still hoped that someone would come along and pick him up and take him to a hospital. He knew he needed treatment for his wounds. But if these two men had ignored his plight and failed to help him, would anyone else be willing to take a chance. He tried to think how they would have perceived him and realized just how ragged and filthy he must look. Would he pick up someone that looked like he did? He wanted to say that of course he would, but he acknowledged that was probably just wishful thinking. He might have reacted just as they did. So maybe he really was on his own and shouldn't expect help.

With that he again struggled to his feet. The pain in his lower back was excruciating. He actually cried out as he finally rose to a standing position. He was positive that the pain came from his spleen and kidneys and he wondered if they could even be healed. Maybe it was impossible. He looked up ahead and started the next leg of his journey. The moon had now fully risen and he heard the baying of coyotes or wolves in the distance, striking even more fear into him.

After about ten paces he saw a broken limb about five feet long on the side of the road. It had fallen from one of the trees on the hillside and he now picked it up to use as a staff. *I'm a shepherd with my staff* he laughed to himself deliriously. The staff seemed to help at first but after another fifty yards, he began to feel lightheaded and dizzy. He stopped and hoped that his head would clear. But instead he fell again to his knees and then crumpled over. This time was different from the others. He felt consciousness slipping away and thought to himself *so this is what it's like to die. Lord, take care of my family and please receive me.* His thoughts then faded away and he lay motionless on the side of the road.

If he had stayed awake just a few seconds longer he would have heard the distant sound of a third vehicle coming toward him on this lonely stretch of road.

# Chapter Seven

Mariachi music echoed loudly from the rusty old black Chevy Silverado pickup and Miguel Alfaro sang loudly and enthusiastically with the lyrics. The bed of the old pickup was loaded with a lawnmower, leaf blower, edger and two 5-gallon gasoline cans. Two bags of weed and feed fertilizer also lay in the bed. He had just finished his day job as a self-employed landscaper and was going to drop off his equipment at home before reporting to his night job. The night job offered secured parking for employees but Miguel didn't like taking a chance. He couldn't afford to lose his equipment or have it stolen.

Miguel was from Venezuela and had come to the United States four years ago. He loved his country but believed it was not a safe place for him and his wife to raise their two sons. He had been happy when Hugo Chavez was first elected President in 1999 and things seemed to improve for the common person at first. But by the end of his term it was becoming evident that corruption reigned higher than economic improvement. Chavez was followed by Nicolas Maduro in 2013 and he had ruled as President, but really dictator, ever since. Since he came to power, hundreds of thousands of Venezuelans had protested over the high levels of criminal violence, corruption, hyperinflation, and chronic scarcity of basic goods. Over five million, like Miguel, had fled the country during that time.

Miguel was an educated man and had been a teacher in the capital city of Caracas. He had resisted the suggestions and examples of many of his friends to leave, but the turning point came when cartel members invaded the home of his neighbor. They kidnapped the family's twelve year old son to serve as a drug mule and then they raped his wife and daughter before his very eyes after beating him nearly to death. The next day Miguel and his family gathered a backpack of belongings each and took what little money they had from the bank and started migrating north.

A fellow teacher who was a close and trusted friend had driven them from Caracas to San Cristobal near the eastern border, but from there they had been afoot. Joining other migrants they crossed Columbia and then Panama, Costa Rica, Nicaragua, Honduras, and Guatemala before finally getting to Mexico. He would have preferred to settle in Mexico, but that government had imposed severe restrictions in the last year and so he, his family and the other migrants in his group made the roughly one thousand mile trek from southern Mexico to the U.S. border where he sought asylum for his family. The entire journey had taken four months. He had lost thirty pounds during that time and his wife had lost twenty five pounds. He wasn't sure how much his children had lost but they were basically skin and bone now.

Once in the U.S. they stayed in a detention facility for a couple of weeks until he was given an address in Phoenix Arizona to which they were to report. They made that trip in a bus provided by a church group and he was given a date to report for a hearing after Miguel filed an application for asylum. Almost a year later the family appeared at the hearing and their application was approved. They could now legally stay and work in the United States. Miguel understood from the immigration lawyer who represented them that they could apply for Permanent Residency in about five years and he had every intention of doing so.

The trip from Venezuela had been excruciating, the legal process to stay in the country had been long and had kept them on edge for that first year. But now came the more difficult part, obtaining work and assimilating into this new culture. Applicants could apply for work permits six months after filing their application. During that six months Miguel had worked as a day laborer doing roofing, mowing, or whatever to earn money. They had stayed in housing provided by a charity initially and then moved in with a family he had gotten to know while working. The kids went to school but struggled with language differences. The entire family worked hard to better their English.

Once he had the work permit he sought more permanent employment. He was not certified to teach in the U.S. and he had taught Spanish and Venezuelan History, which did not meet any job requirements in his new country. He first landed a permanent job with a landscape company. The work was hot and difficult, but that was okay. They weren't getting wealthy, but at least this was a steady income. He then learned of a housekeeping and janitorial job on a night shift. Securing this second job enabled them to move to a moderate but clean apartment where they had one bedroom and the kids another. It was at this time that he quit the landscape company and started working as a self-employed landscaper.

That had been nearly three years ago and they had now settled pretty well into their new life. Each of the boys had school friends and each was on grade level with their learning. They had adapted well to their new language and seldom even spoke Spanish anymore. He and his wife had also made a point to improve their English and made good progress, however not as good as the kids. Though they tried to always speak English at home, they often found themselves resorting to their native tongue.

His wife had gotten a job with a home cleaning service and this had helped bring in additional income that they saved in hopes of buying their own home someday. The family attended a nearby Catholic Church on a regular basis and had made a number of friends there as well. They had attended church in Venezuela also, but now it seemed even more important to them. Miguel had never thought he would end up doing manual labor like he now did, but that was okay. He was grateful and leaned on the knowledge that his sons and his wife were safe and his children would have great opportunities here in their new land. What father wouldn't be willing to sacrifice as he had to guarantee that for his family?

## Chapter Eight

Miguel had just finished a couple of commercial jobs in Kingsville. Both were apartment complexes and he had contracted with each to keep the grounds mowed and the shrubs and flower boxes maintained. The heat had been harsh today and the sweat had rolled over his body. He had finished the last job just as the sun set and was now driving back to his apartment on the outskirts of Garrison. Taking occasional swigs from a cold water bottle, he sang along with the Mariachi song "Volver Volver" which translates to "Come Back, Come Back". It was what was known as a "ranchera" song and it told the story of a man who desired an old flame but faced the impossibility of turning back the clock. Miguel didn't have the best voice but he loved to sing and there was no audience except himself in the old truck. Most of the Mariachi on local radio stations was Mexican in origin instead of Venezuelan, but he had learned to love the songs anyway.

He hoped to get home in time to take a quick shower as well as unload his equipment. With any luck he would also be able to grab a bite of dinner and visit a few moments with his wife and sons. The biggest downside to holding down two jobs was not having enough time with his family and he regretted that terribly, but knew in the long run it would be worth it.

The last apartment had been a block from the old highway and so he decided to take that route tonight. Normally he would have preferred the interstate but going back to it would take extra time so this seemed like the shortest route this evening. He took it slowly around the curves and bends of the road, not wanting his equipment to roll around in the bed. The one thing he was thankful for was that he encountered no traffic coming from the other direction. There was also no one behind him most of the time until a new Ford Edge SUV roared into view in his mirror.

The Edge was obviously going faster than him and wanted to pass but that was not easy on this road. Finally, after the Edge had followed him for a mile or so he had enough room on the shoulder to pull over slightly and let the SUV pass him. The man driving the Edge sped past him and waved has he pulled in front of Miguel to express his gratitude. *At least he was polite and it wasn't a one-fingered salute* Miguel laughed to himself.

He drove another three or four miles, still singing along to the music, when he navigated an especially sharp curve. As he exited the curve his headlights shone on an object on the shoulder that gave him pause. *Que hay en el mundo? What in the world?* At first he didn't know what to make of what he was seeing, but then he realized it was a man in the road. The man lay motionless as he approached and stopped his truck. *Esta muerto? Is he dead?* He muttered this to himself in Spanish. He then got out of the truck and ran over to the seemingly lifeless body. Turning the man over, he saw that it was a white man and that he had obviously been badly beaten. He looked around now, fearing that whoever had done this might be lying in wait to attack him as well. But he saw no one lurking in the bushes and quickly turned his attention back to the man in his arms. He then noticed blood clotted on the top of the man's head and took out his handkerchief and looped it around the top of the head and around the chin to secure it. He didn't know if that helped or not, but it was all he could think to do.

Miguel opened the passenger door on his truck and then grabbed the water bottle and ran back to the man. Pouring a little water over his face and a tiny amount in his mouth, he saw the man opened his eyes a little. He looked at Miguel and then groaned while trying to say something. Miguel rejoiced that the stranger was alive and wrapped his arms underneath the arms of the man. He dragged him to the truck and was starting to lift him into the cab when he seemed to awaken again and helped push himself into the truck. Miguel got in the driver's side and lifted the water botte so the man could get another drink.

Miguel fastened the stranger in with the seat belt and said "Hold on Senor, I take you to hospital." The man looked at him through still groggy eyes and quietly whispered "Thank you". Pressing the accelerator Miguel now picked up his speed and rushed as fast as the old truck would go toward Garrison. He could hear the lawnmower and other equipment rolling around in the back, but now was not the time to be careful. He wasn't sure which town was closer at this point but he knew where the hospital was in Garrison and thought it was probably better equipped.

While they were gliding down the road, the man seemed to regain more consciousness. As they approached the edge of Garrison, Miguel realized that his own apartment was only two blocks away, but going there now was not an option. This stranger was seriously hurt and needed help as soon as possible. He wondered how he had ended up on the roadside like that. Had he been walking? Had someone hijacked his car? How was that possible on a highway like that? These questions raced through his mind as he drew nearer and nearer to the hospital. Finally they arrived at the facility and Miguel went to the Emergency Room entrance. He ran inside and told a security guard that he had a badly injured man in his truck. The security guard called one of the ER Doctors and a nurse over and they all ran outside. Lifting Bryan onto a gurney they prepared to take him inside, but Bryan stopped them. He then mustered up the energy to ask if Miguel had a cell phone and Miguel said that he did. He gave him a number and said "Please sir, call my wife and tell her." Miguel assured him that he would.

He made the call and then looked at the time on his iPhone. He still had time to go home and unload his equipment, but there would be no shower or dinner tonight. Maybe he would get a vending machine sandwich after clocking in at work.

## Chapter Nine

He could feel something touching him, pulling at him, nudging him. Was it the coyotes or the wolves? Did they sense his death? Had they come to finish him off and rip him apart, fighting each other as they devoured him? He was aware of being touched, but still not fully conscious as he sensed his body being rolled over so that he was on his back. Then he heard a voice saying "Hey, Senor are you okay? What's happened to you?"

He slowly opened his eyes a little and squinted at the man looking down at him. His first thought was that the brown skinned man had stumbled upon him and would rob him of whatever he had left. The man then said something that sounded like *Esta muerto?* Bryan spoke no Spanish but thought *muerto* meant dead. Yes, the man was going to kill him. But then the man said in a gentle whisper something about taking him to the hospital. *Oh, praise the Lord! Thank you!* The man then grabbed Bryan by his arms and started pulling him to an old beat up truck. He could feel the man trying to lift him into the cab and managed to push a little with his own legs to help him. Soon they were both in the cab and the man gave Bryan a drink. Water never tasted so good! He tried to tell the driver to go to Garrison but couldn't muster the words as he drifted off to near unconsciousness again.

He seemed to somehow sense the bumpiness of the road and swaying back and forth around the curves as the old pickup sped toward the hospital. Then the door suddenly opened and people were picking him up and lying him down on a gurney. He came to again and suddenly thought of his family, Andrea and Aaron. Andrea must be worried sick, and he needed her here with him. He again called upon all his strength and asked the stranger to call her. He told the stranger his name was Bryan and he gave the man her number. The man replied in broken English that he would call her immediately. Then they rushed him inside the Emergency Room.

It seemed to him that the ER was in a state of organized chaos. He heard terms being spoken all around him like "stat" and "contusion" and "hemorrhaging". Words he had heard before but didn't really know what they meant. There were also strange words that scared him more like "intracranial hematoma" and "nephralgia". What the heck did that mean? He had no idea but then they rushed him to an operating room and the unconsciousness returned, but this time it was induced by anesthesia.

Sometime later Bryan began to awaken. He didn't know how long it had been but it seemed like days ago when he got the flat tire. Now he batted his eyes open and saw the most beautiful and wonderful sight in the world. Andrea was standing beside his bed holding his hand. When he opened his eyes she let out a cry and said in a halting, teary voice "Oh my God, he's awake". She then came up and held his cheeks in her hands and kissed him over and over. Tears ran down her own cheeks. "I couldn't believe it when that man called. I left Aaron with the Robinsons and rushed over here, but you were already in surgery."

Bryan found his voice, "I'm so glad you're here. I thought I was going to die and all I could think of was you and Aaron. I love you both so much!" A nurse then knocked on the door and came in, interrupting their reunion. She took his vitals and said the doctor would be in soon to see him. On the way out the door she turned towards them and looked at Bryan. "You are one lucky fellow" she said and left the room.

A few minutes later the doctor appeared. "Hello, Bryan is it? I'm Dr. Fellows. I did the surgery." He introduced himself to Andrea and then continued. "Bryan, you took a terrible beating. You're lucky to have survived it, but there was considerable damage. Some of it is permanent. Your left side kidney was practically destroyed and we had to remove it. It was beyond repair, but luckily your other kidney is in good condition. Your spleen was also ravaged and initially we thought it would have to be removed as well, but it should heal. That's good because while you could live without a spleen, you would be much more susceptible to infection and disease for the rest of your life. Finally, the skull fracture is the best news. The blow you took there required several stiches but there was no internal damage to the arteries. The skull should heal itself but we will monitor it frequently and closely to make sure the bone is ossifying and mending properly. That could take six to eight weeks. Any questions?"

Bryan was trying to absorb all the doctor had said. *Any questions? Yes, like why did this happen? But he said,* "That's a lot to take in. I'm sure I'll have questions, but nothing right now. I can't thank you enough, Doctor." Andrea added, "Bless you and all the nurses and everyone. Thank you so much." The doctor seemed somewhat embarrassed to receive such praise and said he would check on him again later and left.

Just when he thought they might have some time alone and he could rest, a deputy from the Sheriff's Department came into the room asking for a statement. He recalled for the deputy his trip earlier that day to Kingsville and his dinner at the diner. Then he explained how he had started home and had a flat tire. With no cell service on the old highway, he had fixed the flat himself and was almost done when the three young men drove up behind him. He detailed how they surrounded him and then attacked, hitting and kicking him over and over. He gave the best description of them that he could, estimating their height and weight. All three were white men. He described their looks including beards, mustaches, hair color, everything he remembered but he doubted it was enough to help very much. The deputy wrote it all down and said they would be in touch with more questions or any new developments. He then left.

Bryan was getting so tired at this point he just wanted to sleep. He closed his eyes as Andrea held his hand. She said that she would bring Aaron to see him tomorrow. He was nearly asleep when he heard someone come into the room. He opened his eyes, assuming it was the nurse or doctor again. But no, it was just a man who appeared to be a janitor. He wondered what was so urgent that the janitor had to enter the room and interrupt his rest. *This is getting irritating* he thought to himself.

# Chapter Ten

Bryan was dead tired and couldn't believe the janitor had something to do in his room that couldn't wait. He started to say something when the man said in broken English, "Hello Senor, I want just to know you okay". Suddenly a distant sense of recognition struck Bryan and he looked at Andrea and said, "Oh my God Andrea this is him, the man who saved me!" Without hesitation she dropped Bryan's hand and rushed to Miguel and threw her arms around him. "Oh thank you, sir! Thank you! I can't thank you enough! I'm so glad you called me. You saved my husband's life!"

Miguel was not a person who normally welcomed hugs and touching. He was pretty timid about physical contact but he allowed the woman to hug him and then gently pulled away. "I only do the right" he said. She hugged him again before Miguel could step away and she even kissed his cheek. Bryan now spoke up, "Yes sir, thank you so much. I had given up hope".

"You better now?" Miguel asked.

"Yes, they say I'm going to be okay thanks to you. I don't know how to ever repay you." Then Bryan held out his hand and Miguel didn't seem to understand at first, but then he strode forward to the side of the bed and shook hands with Bryan. "What is your name, sir?" Bryan asked and Miguel simply replied with his first name. "Miguel, thank you again. Thank you so much."

Obviously nervous, Miguel now backed away towards the door. "Nurse say only five minutes so I go now." As he reached the door Bryan said "Okay, but please come see me again tomorrow, okay? I mean it." Miguel nodded and responded simply "Si Senor" as he left the room.

Looking at Andrea he said "If he doesn't come by on his own, you hunt him down tomorrow." She promised that she would do just that and added, "Now, you go to sleep Mister. I'll be right here when you wake up." She then kissed him and watched him close his eyes. In no time at all he was sound asleep.

He slept about four hours before the nurse came in and checked his vital signs again. She also checked his bandages to make sure they were snugly attached. A few minutes later Dr. Fellows came in and examined him. He assured them both that all looked good and that he would see him again tomorrow. He then asked Bryan if he wanted a mild sedative to help him sleep, which Bryan refused. Sleeping was the one thing he could do now with little effort.

Morning comes early in hospitals and about 7:00 AM a new nurse entered the room, making her rounds. This woke up both him and Andrea. Andrea said she was going to get Aaron and bring him by the hospital. He would miss the morning session of his first grade class, but she thought seeing his daddy was more important.

He had just finished breakfast when he heard a knock on the door and his pastor came in. Pastor Jacobs said he was shocked to hear what had happened to Bryan and wanted him to know that he and the rest of the church would be praying for him. He asked about the incident, which Bryan related to him, and also asked what the prognosis was for Bryan's health. He was genuinely concerned and Bryan really appreciated his visit. He took Bryan's hand and was saying a prayer when the door burst open and Aaron came in yelling "Daddy, Daddy!" He saw that the men were praying and said "Oh, sorry". They finished the prayer and both men had to fight to keep from laughing at the interruption. Bryan ached as he laughed but it was worth every bit of the pain.

Aaron stayed for a couple of hours. He was noticeably scared by the surroundings and his dad's condition at first, but was feeling much better by the time he left. Andrea took him to school and then went home. There were some things she needed to do. She promised him they both would return when school was out.

Bryan slept a good bit of the afternoon until about 4:00 PM when the two returned. When Andrea came into the room she said, "I saw Miguel in the hallway and reminded him to come see you again. He promised he would." Indeed Miguel stuck his head in the door about twenty minutes later, just as shyly as he had the first time. Bryan waved him in and said, "Aaron, this is Miguel. Miguel saved your daddy's life yesterday. He's a wonderful person." Aaron ran and hugged the taller Miguel around the waist saying, "Thank you Miguel, Thank you Miguel" over and over. Finally he let go and Miguel came over and shook Bryan's hand. After updating Miguel on his condition Bryan looked him intently in the eye and said "Miguel why did you stop for me yesterday? Two different people slowed down and stopped and then sped away. They were scared. Scared of being attacked, scared of me, repulsed by me; I don't know what they thought but they both left me there. Why did you stop?"

Miguel heard the question and understood the gist of it. He wished one of his sons was here to translate for him. He struggled for the words and finally said "I think you say Rule of Gold." Bryan didn't understand what he was trying to convey but Andrea picked up on it. "You mean The Golden Rule, Miguel?" "Si Si! He then said "Mi madre, my mother, she say treat people like you want them treat you."

Bryan then said "we say it like this: Do unto others as you would have them do unto you".

"Si! Si! That is it, Senor". He thought for a minute and reached into his pocket and pulled out a small book. It was a New Testament that a group called the Gideons had given to hospital staff. His was in Spanish. "My mother say it is also in Bible" and he turned to Matthew 7:12. Andrea walked to an end table by

Bryan's bed and opened a drawer. An English Bible had been placed in the room by that same group of men. She turned to the gospel of Matthew and read the verse Miguel had indicated:

"Therefore, whatever you want men to do to you, do also to them, for this is the Law and the Prophets."

They talked for a few more minutes and then Miguel excused himself, saying he had to return to work. Bryan was very quiet after that and after several minutes Andrea asked, "Are you okay? What's wrong?" Bryan took a deep breath and said, "I think this has changed me." Andrea replied, "Of course it has, but you'll get well; you'll be okay."

"No." he said. "You don't understand. I was just thinking that if the situation was reversed, I probably wouldn't have stopped for Miguel. I would have seen a brown-skinned man lying there and figured he was a gang member or an illegal or something and just drove on, just like those two people did to me. But now, I'm seeing things differently. We have to live just like that verse says. We can't ignore people. We have to have compassion."

Bryan was released from the hospital a week later. The first thing he did was find out where Miguel lived. Over time the two families became close and visited each other often. Miguel's sons help Aaron learn to throw and catch a baseball. Andrea and Miguel's wife got together occasionally for lunch. Miguel taught Bryan a little Spanish and Bryan helped Miguel with his English. And Bryan worked hard to change his perspective and live according to that Golden Rule. He taught Aaron to have compassion on those in need and to judge people according to the content of their hearts and not just their appearance and circumstances. Those things were temporary, but the heart is permanent.

# Epilogue

So, did you guess correctly that The Unexpected is based on the parable of the Good Samaritan found in Luke 10:30-37? This is probably one of the best known and most loved of the parables told by Jesus. It tells us about a tragic event that befell another human being and how some of the people we would most expect to offer help chose instead to ignore the man's plight.

At its heart this is a simple yet profound story of basic human decency. It's always heartening when tragedies like hurricanes or tornadoes strike and we see people doing all they can to aid and assist their fellow men and women. They don't ask about their politics or their ethnicity or their position in society at these times. They simply help. Sadly there are also many other times when we fail to show that same compassion for very shallow and misguided reasons.

Let us all remember and be encouraged by this tale of the Good Samaritan. Let us serve and help our neighbors not out of obligation but because it's simply the right thing to do. It's what Jesus would have done.

# The
# Rescue

*by*
*Bobby J Watson*

"God is on the move to rescue people from misery to everlasting happiness, which can only be found in him."

-John Piper

# Chapter One

"Where is he? I haven't seen him since Friday." Eric posed the question to Jacob as the two sat at a table in the club. The club was not what you might expect, but just a large room with some tables and chairs with a concrete floor and white plaster walls. The walls were decorated haphazardly and sometimes there was live music, but there was no dancing, no drinking, and no bar. It wasn't that kind of club. This club was just a place where like-minded people with a common bond gathered and supported each other.

"Don't you know?" responded Jacob as the two sat at a table facing each other. "Know what? No, obviously I don't."

"Paula has disappeared and he's gone to find her. She's been missing for a week now and no one knows where she went. So he left Friday to find her and we haven't heard anything from either of them since then."

"Oh, okay. I didn't know. Actually I only met Paula a couple of times. She's fairly new I think."

"Yeah, she came on board about a month ago. Seems like a nice person, but has her baggage."

Jacob grinned ever so slightly, "Haven't we all, my friend? Haven't we all?" He then went on, "I've seen this before. He'll be back and assuming Paula is alive, she'll be with him. No matter how long it takes."

"Yeah, I've heard people say that before. Still, I miss him. James does a good job, but he's just not Adam. I'll be glad when he finds the girl and gets back here."

Adam was the leader of the club and everyone loved him. Everyone had a story about how Adam had encountered them at some point in their life and how he had led them to the club.

James was Adam's brother and he assisted Adam and substituted for him whenever Adam was absent. Just as Eric said, James was a good leader in his own right. Everyone respected him but Adam simply had a charisma that was unmatched and there was no real substitute for him.

James had gone through a lot himself earlier in his life. It wasn't easy being the brother of Adam. Living in his shadow had been its own kind of torture and torment. From the time he was born Adam had seemed like the perfect child and then the perfect teen and then the perfect adult. James was two years his junior and could never live up to the standard Adam set so he had taken his own path. He was rebellious in school and spent more time in the principal's office than in the classroom. If he wasn't mouthing off to the teacher, he was picking a fight with a fellow student at recess. As he entered his teen years he fell in with a group that taught him the escape that alcohol provided. Wanting more he tried his first drugs when he was fourteen and started shoplifting and petty theft to support his growing habit.

He was sixteen when he stole a car and led the police on a wild joy ride through a residential neighborhood before wrecking the car. He went to juvenile court and his mother pleaded with the judge and asked him to give the boy one more chance. The judge agreed since it was his first offense, but two weeks later he was before that same judge again for breaking into a neighbor's home and stealing their jewelry and a television. A Ring camera captured him entering and leaving the house. This time the judge gave him six months at a juvenile detention center. This turned out to be the best school he had ever attended as other boys shared their criminal expertise and techniques with him.

So it was no surprise when he joined a gang after leaving detention and soon he was not only using drugs but selling them as well. The gang also taught him how to hot wire cars and sell them to a chop shop that disassembled them and sold the parts. He quickly gained the admiration of other members and for the first time in his life he felt respected.

Despite this apparent success however, James felt hollow inside and saw no purpose in his life. He felt lonely all the time, even when surrounded by his so-called friends in the gang. This was only intensified whenever his mother invited him to dinner or he was around the family for a birthday or some other celebration. Everyone just seemed to have something that he did not possess and he didn't understand it. Adam worked as a roofer and general construction worker for a company building houses. He made nothing like the money that James made, but he seemed to get by and more importantly he was always happy. Not giddy happy, but something else, something deeper. Contentment. That's what it was.

Things took a turn one year when they were both in their mid-twenties and the family had gathered for Christmas. They had a nice dinner and then exchanged gifts, just as they had done every Christmas and then everyone settled back and engaged in conversation. James was feeling especially lost and lonely that year and soon he stepped out on the back porch. Lost in his thoughts he didn't notice that Adam had followed him until he said, "You don't seem like yourself tonight, James." James started to make some excuse but his emotions got the better of him and he started to sob. "I don't know, Adam. I'm just tired of trying. I feel empty, pointless. I feel like just giving up." With his guard down he asked Adam for the first time, "What keeps you going? You always seem so happy."

Adam then explained that his life was built around and resided in an abiding faith in God. He explained that no one was perfect but that if you asked God in faith he would forgive us our mistakes, no matter what they were, and give meaning to our life. He had a job for each of us if we just accepted him into our life and sought that purpose.

"It sounds too easy" James said as he listened. "And you have no idea the things I've done."

"Doesn't matter" Adam responded. "God is big enough and generous enough to forgive anything. We just have to have the faith and be brave enough to ask him. And brother, let me ask you this: what do you have to lose? Try it."

"How do I do that?"

Then right there on the back porch Adam asked James to kneel and led him in a prayer as James acknowledged his faith in God.

Soon after that James left the gang and became a car salesman. He had the gift of gab and proved to be a good salesman. For the first time in his life he began to believe that he had value and he felt that contentment and fulfillment he had seen in others. Emily worked in the office at the dealership and they began dating and were married a year later. Life was good and he had Adam to thank for it.

It was soon after his marriage that Adam approached him one evening at home and said, "James I have something in mind. Something that will help others find their purpose, find peace and fulfillment. I need your help. Will you help me?"

The club was born at that moment. James had no idea what Adam had in mind but he knew that his brother had a remarkable relationship with God and that it had to be something worthwhile. Maybe this was the job God had in mind for him.

## Chapter Two

Adam got out of his car and stood in front of the small, white frame house. He thought about what to say as he approached the front door and knocked on it. This was a part of his mission that was absolutely essential, but it was also the part he could never enjoy and dreaded the most. Still he was hopeful as he waited at the door. He heard some movement within and soon a man opened the door. The man was probably in his early to mid-fifties. He stood about 5'11" and was of medium build. His once brown hair was now mostly white and he had a kind but tired demeanor as he said, "Yes, can I help you?"

"Hello sir, I'm Adam Shepherd. I don't know if Paula has ever mentioned me but I'm a friend of hers. I wonder if I could come in for a minute."

The man seemed to sigh inwardly and opened the door wider to let him in. As he did so, he called for his wife "Sally, there's someone here about Paula."

Sally came into the room wearing an apron. She was about the age of the man and a foot shorter with gray hair. She was wringing her hands and had the look of someone whose life had been consumed by worry.

They invited him to sit and Adam again explained, "I'm a friend of Paula's. I met her a few months ago and we became friends. In fact she joined a group of us, who get together pretty often, but she has disappeared and I've been looking for her. Have you seen or heard from her lately?"

"Why would we hear from her? What kind of group? Is this some kind of cult or something?"

"Oh no sir, we're not a cult, not at all. We are believers but nothing like that. Our group just leans on each other for support and guidance. We care about each other. Since you're her parents I thought maybe she had told you about us, or maybe told you where she was going."

Sally now spoke, "Oh my. I would be so happy if she's found friends like you describe. In the past she's just found people who use and abuse her. We've tried to get help for her, but it never works. It's almost like she hates us for even trying."

The two of them now told Adam about the Paula they knew. The dad did most of the talking with Sally occasionally adding to what he said. Paula had been raised in a loving home and had been a normal, happy girl growing up. She was a good student in school and had been a cheerleader for youth football teams and then for her junior high and high school. Her friends had lived similar lives and they would have overnight bunk parties and birthday bashes and all the things that defined middle-class America.

It was her senior year in high school when things started to change. She met a boy named Luther who seemed like a nice enough young man, but looks are deceiving. First they learned that he had enticed her to drink alcohol and then to smoke marijuana. She started staying out past her curfew and then staying out all night. They tried to discourage her from seeing Luther but that only made her more determined. When they finally grounded her, even though she was now seventeen, she sneaked out the window and saw him anyway.

She barely managed to graduate and went away to college. They hoped that would end her relationship with Luther but in fact she never attended classes. Instead she lived in the dormitory but spent all her time with Luther, who enrolled in the same school. She failed the first semester and then dropped out, moving into a shabby little apartment with him. Her parents tried to visit but she barely made time for them. A few months later she became pregnant and had a miscarriage because she refused to quit drinking and doing drugs for the baby's sake. By then she had moved on to other, more potent and lethal drugs.

Luther in the meantime grew tired of her and started seeing other women. Shattered by this, she attempted suicide. The hospital notified her parents who rushed to her side. She seemed happy to see them this time and even moved back home, but it only lasted a short while until she was back on drugs and soon left with another man she had met. That was three years ago and was the last time they had seen or heard from her. They had attempted to find her whereabouts but never succeeded. Finally they gave up and faced the reality that they had lost her. Since that day they had never ceased praying that she would come back to them.

"That pretty much is the same story she told me when I first met her" said Adam. "I can tell you that she still loves you and she told me about growing up here. That's how I knew where you lived."

"Please tell us about her" Sally pleaded. "We miss her so much. We've prayed so long".

Adam again explained that he had met Paula a few months earlier. "I have to tell you that when I met Paula, it was not good. She was in an awful situation, one that you can't even imagine."

He then told them that he had first encountered Paula in the downtown area of the large city about twenty miles away. He had met some friends for dinner at a popular restaurant and had parked a few blocks away in a public parking lot. When returning to his car he heard a noise in an alleyway and then he heard a female voice yelling "No! No! Give it back!" He rushed into the dark alley and found a man and woman. The man had a handful of money and was pushing the woman back against the brick wall of a building. When he saw Adam he ran the opposite way and out of the alley, while Adam stopped to see if the woman was okay. He started to call 911 on his cell phone when the woman stopped him. "No, don't do that" she said in a loud voice and then added "It would just end up getting me busted again". He then

49

understood that she was a prostitute and the man had stolen back his money after their "transaction" was completed.

He introduced himself and she said that her name was Paula. He invited her to come with him where she could clean up and have a safe, warm place to sleep if she needed it. She understood this to mean he wanted to take advantage of her services and said "Sure, why not". Instead he took her to the club where she met a few other people who were there that night. She showered and then he showed her a room with cots where she could sleep. She seemed reluctant at first, not trusting anyone, but soon she lay down and was fast asleep.

The next morning when she awakened another man, Adam's brother James, made breakfast for her. As she enjoyed eggs and pancakes with orange juice and coffee, Adam asked about her background. She was not ready to open up and gave him little information, but that was okay. He was used to that. He then did something totally unexpected. He gave her a little book, a New Testament, and asked her if she knew that God loved her. She accepted the book but laughed and said "Nobody loves me except maybe my parents and I've totally let them down". She left soon after finishing her meal, but Adam told her she could return whenever she wanted.

He didn't see her again for a few weeks, but then she showed up one night and slept there again. This time she met a few other members of the club and heard their stories. She then began to periodically appear for a night or even two or three in a row. Each time she engaged more with the others who were there and spent more time talking with James and Adam. Finally one night Adam asked her if she had been reading the New Testament and she said she had. He then asked her if she believed God loved her. She thought about this and then said very quietly, "You know, I do believe that now". He then led her in a prayer of repentance as she accepted God into her life.

"That sounds so wonderful", exclaimed Sally. "But you said she's missing now?"

"Yes, she started coming regularly to the club and she even got a job at a local restaurant as a hostess. Things seemed to be really turning around for her and then she disappeared. I thought nothing of it when she missed a few nights but after a week I went to the restaurant. They said she had skipped out on her job too. That's when I started trying to find her."

He gave them a card with his cell number and encouraged them to call if they heard from her. He also got their number and promised to update them with any news.

The dad now looked at Adam. His eyes were moist and his voice broke as he said, "Please sir, find my little girl".

Adam looked at them both and said "I want you to know that I won't stop looking until I find her."

# Chapter Three

Paula woke up shivering with cold and looked up at the ceiling in the shabby little motel room. The ceiling had water stains marking it in several places and the walls were a combination of peeling plaster and dark brown stains. She didn't want to think about what caused those stains. She lay there for several minutes with her mind in a fog before her memory refreshed. She couldn't believe what had happened and where she now found herself. She thought she had left this life behind. Life with her new friends had been so good the last few months and she had left behind her addictions and the things she had to do to support those addictions. Her life had taken on meaning and while it wasn't the greatest job, her hostess position had enabled her to live in a small but decent apartment. Why did she find herself back here?

She got up and started putting on her clothes when she suddenly stopped and looked around the little room. She checked the bathroom and found it empty. She remembered now that a man had come here with her. What was his name, Joe? John? She barely recalled what he looked like much less what his name was. He had approached her in a sleazy bar and they had ended up here. As she thought about it, she hung her head and started to cry. Why was she back here, in this life? Her thoughts then turned to the club and to Adam. One thing she knew for sure was that she didn't want Adam to find her like this. Then she thought of her parents. She had almost been ready to reconnect with them, and now this.

Her thoughts returned to Adam. He had led her to a new life. She had never met anyone like him. Oh, the world was full of do-gooders and even kind people, but he was different. He was so genuine. You somehow knew that he really cared about you and that he only had your best interest in mind. It was hard to explain but when you looked into his eyes you were transported to a new level. You wanted to have a real purpose. You wanted to live life like the gift it was, with thankfulness and gratitude. You wanted to be pure in thought and deed. You wanted to be like him.

Well, she certainly wasn't fulfilling any of that now was she? How had she ended up back in this life? She sat on the bed, lost in her thoughts. She had been working at that restaurant and everything seemed okay. Then one night a man came in and when she asked how many in his party he opted to eat at the counter. But he kept looking at her and finally said, "Remember me, honey?" She said she didn't but he persisted. "How could you forget me, baby? We had a couple of swell nights together." He was obviously a john she had dealt with in her past but there were so many, how would she remember just one? She turned red with embarrassment and hoped he would go away soon.

When he finished eating he approached her and said quietly, "Listen babe, what time do you get off? Tell you what. I'll pick you up and we'll have a good time and then I'll forget you. Otherwise I may have to spread the word around here about you."

She didn't know what to do. She didn't want to go with him but she didn't want to be exposed for her past either. Finally she told him what time she got off and agreed to meet him, just this once. He left and she waited and watched the clock the rest of the evening. She had lied about when her shift ended. She actually got off thirty minutes earlier than she told him and when that time came she left. She was in a panic and just wanted to get away. She should have gone to the club but she didn't want to disappoint Adam and the other members. She wasn't ready for all the members to know the details of her past. So she ran to her apartment to hide.

Instead of settling down once there, she grew more panicky. What had she gotten herself into? Who was she fooling? She was just a worthless tramp, nothing more. She needed something to calm her nerves. Before long she was on the street, going to where her dealer often hung out. If he wasn't there, someone would know where he was. She just needed one hit to settle her nerves. At least that's what she told herself. She found her old dealer who was more than glad to accommodate her. Just one time she told herself, but she knew that was a lie.

She returned to her apartment that night. The next day was payday and she went by the restaurant and picked up her check. It was two days until her rent was due, but she didn't pay it, instead taking her few clothes and checking into a motel. This one was fairly nice, but she knew she couldn't afford to stay there long. She was slowly accepting her new reality. Her attempt to live a normal life, a life that Adam would approve had failed. She knew that first relapse with drugs was not her last one. She knew she was back in the life. But where could she go? She didn't want Adam or anyone else in the club to find her or even accidentally spot her here. There must be somewhere she could go. Should she leave the city? She really had never spent much time anywhere else so going somewhere new was a scary proposition. But she couldn't stay around here.

Ever since she had first left home she had lived in the downtown area of the city. This was where she had frequented the dive bars, met her dealer, and lived her life. The club was even close to downtown. But she knew it was a large city and the south side was reputed to be even more sordid and disreputable than downtown. She could go there and hide. No one would come looking for her there. And so, now homeless with a duffel bag of clothes and nothing else, she began walking south down one of the main thoroughfares of the city. Tears began to roll down her cheeks as she trudged along. She didn't really want this. She had found happiness like she had never known the last few weeks. Why had that guy come into the restaurant?

She thought about the club as she walked. That had been a wonderful experience for her. Everyone had been so nice there. Everyone just wanted to reach their potential, to fulfill the purpose that God had for them. No one was out to take what they could. No one was there to take advantage of anyone else. She had never known that such a place existed. A smile came to her face as she thought about James and Adam. What a couple of guys they were. Then her thoughts turned to her parents. They had been good parents. They had never shown her anything but love and they had provided for her to the best of their abilities. She remembered how her dad always called her "Paulie girl" like it was one name. She couldn't help but giggle a little.

All these people had been so good to her. And how had she repaid them? Yes, it was better that they think her dead than to find her and be disappointed.

# Chapter Four

Jason walked down the sidewalk toward the club. It was a hot, sweltering summer day and with evening coming the humidity was so high it felt like you could hold a cloth in the air and wring the water from it. He had worked some long hours lately and hadn't been to the club for a few days. He missed it. He missed the comradery of his friends there and the support they gave him.

He reached the building and walked inside. There seemed to be a pretty good crowd tonight and James met him at the door, "Hey brother, it's good to see you. We've missed you lately." Jason shook his hand and gave him a hug, "Good to see you too, James. Is Adam here tonight?" James explained Adam's absence and assured Jason he would be back soon. "I have no doubt of that" replied Jason as he walked on inside the room. Seeing Roberto sitting alone at a table he took a seat across from him.

"Hola" said Roberto standing up and giving Jason a hug. "Hola yourself" answered Jason. Roberto had been born in the Dominican Republic but had moved to the US with his parents when he was four years old. He spoke English with no discernable accent, but he liked to throw in a little of his native tongue occasionally. Jason spoke just enough Spanish to play along with him. "So I hear that Adam is out scouring the city for Paula" he said.

"Si, that's what I heard too."

"Well, if anyone can find her it's Adam. I don't know how he does it but he just always seems to know where we are when we need help. Where did he find you, Roberto?"

"Oh, I thought I had told you this story before, but maybe not." Roberto then went on to describe his first encounter with Adam.

"My story is not as dramatic as a lot of the people here, kind of plain and boring actually. I was always sort of a loner, maybe because of my heritage or my broken English when I was younger. I don't know why but I just never had close friends like most kids and that followed me on through high school and afterward. I was working as a cashier at a convenience store, just making a wage and filling my time. There was nothing exciting about it, nothing rewarding. It was just a job and I was pretty bored most of the time. I knew the other employees at the store, but again no real relationships. Life was pretty much just a drag, you know? A lot of nights when I got off work I would go to this bar and sit at the bar and have a beer or two. I wasn't an alcoholic or anything. I hardly ever even got a buzz, but I would sit there and watch others come and go and just past the time. My parents had died in a car accident and it beat going home to an empty apartment.

One night I'm sitting there like usual drinking a beer when the time comes to go home. I was scheduled to work the early shift the next day so I was leaving a little earlier than usual. When I walked outside, Adam was there. It was like he was waiting for me, even though I had never seen him in my life. He looked at me and asked, 'Wouldn't you rather sit with friends instead of in there by yourself?' I started to tell him that I didn't know him and he should mind his own business, but there was just something so sincere and genuine about him. I had never met anyone like him, so I told him that would be nice but I didn't really have any friends around here. I was ashamed to say I didn't have any friends anywhere else either. He said 'come with me and I'll introduce you to some'. With most people I would have thought it was some kind of setup to mug me or something but like I said he was different so I followed him.

That was my first trip to the club. I went back to the bar a time or two, but then I started going to the club after work every day instead. Soon I was learning about God and how he loved me.

I felt like part of something for the first time. The rest as they say is history."

"That's quite a story, actually."

"So what's your story, Jason?"

"I guess you could say that mine is more dramatic, but it's really very similar. When I was twenty three years old me and another guy robbed a liquor store. We didn't hurt anyone but we did have guns. I guess we weren't too good at being robbers because they caught us on video and arrested us for armed robbery the next day. It was my first offense and I got five to ten in state prison. You think having no friends was bad, you should try prison. You constantly have to watch your back in that place. The least little wrong move or word can get you an enemy coming for you. Anyway, I got out on parole after five years and three months. Then the darnedest thing happened.

When I walked out of prison that day I was going to catch a bus to the city. My dad died from a heart attack and my mom from COVID while I was in the joint so there was no one there to pick me up or anything. At least that's what I thought. But when I walked to the bus stop, Adam was standing there. I had never seen the man in my life, but there he was and he said 'Well I'll bet you're glad to be out of there'. I was thinking who is this guy? I decided he must have just assumed I had come from the prison since it was close by and I said 'Yeah, you bet'. Then he really shocked me. He said, 'you're gonna need a job. Come with me and I'll help you with one.'

He was right of course. I did need a job and so I went with him. Like you said earlier I wouldn't have done this for anyone else, but he just was different somehow so I tagged along with him. We took his car downtown to an auto repair business. Again, I don't know how he knew but I had learned a little about mechanics in prison. He introduced me to the owner who hired me on the spot. I couldn't believe it! One hour out of prison and I had a job. Then he shocked me again when said 'You'll need a place to stay until you start getting paid'. That's when he took me to the club. I stayed there in a room with some cots and a shower for the first month until I had the money for an apartment.

While I was staying at the club I met several of the members. I learned that the auto shop owner came to the club too. That's how Adam knew him. Like you said I started meeting people and listening to their stories and for the first time I started thinking that maybe there was a God and maybe he did care about me. After I got the apartment I kept coming back there. I didn't want to hang out in bars and end up violating my parole somehow or getting mixed up with the wrong people, and this seemed like a safe harbor. I guess I was a little more stubborn than you. It took me about six months of this before I broke down one night and accepted God into my life. Best decision I ever made."

"Wow! Some story" said Roberto. "Best decision I ever made too."

"I wonder what made Paula leave. She seemed to really be doing well and making progress."

"I don't know amigo, but if anyone can find her and bring her back, it's Adam."

"Got that right, dude."

# Chapter Five

Adam walked down another alley in the downtown area. The city had a large downtown and unlike some cities, this downtown was thriving with shops, bars, theaters and was simply a bustle of activity all day and into the night. He had walked several streets now and nearly as many alleys looking for Paula. So far his only reward was tired legs and sore feet, but he knew that he had to keep going for her sake. Paula had been doing well and had seemed to make good progress. He didn't know what had happened to make her disappear but he knew that no one was beyond redemption and rehabilitation and it was that knowledge that kept him going at times like this. She wasn't the first member to disappear and he knew she wouldn't be the last either. That was just part of his mission and so far he had always found those who wandered away and brought them back into the fold.

The whole idea behind the club had actually started with his brother James. When James abandoned his old life and accepted God that had been a wonderful day, a day they had celebrated. But Adam quickly saw that James needed more, something to bolster his new life and provide essential support. He started attending a church and that was good. He learned more about God, about the Bible, and more about how he should live his life for God. But church was only there part of the week and there were many times, especially at first, when he simply needed something or someone and no one was at the church. Adam had watched his brother and saw this need and after much prayer had formulated this idea about the club. It would be a place that was always open, where people could always come to find the support, the peace, the purpose that they needed.

He pitched the idea to his brother and they started the club. It was just the club. There was no fancy name for it, just the club. Adam knew some other new believers plus a handful of people who had returned to the faith and he recruited them as the first members. God's handiwork in it was evident from the beginning as one of these founding members owned a building downtown that had a large basement room that was ideal for setting up tables, chairs and a stage. He offered it to the club and had Adam sign a 99-year lease on the room for the nominal sum of $1.00 per year. He then gave Adam a $100 bill, which Adam quickly returned. The man then gave Adam a receipt showing it was fully paid for the next century.

Tables and chairs were purchased as they could afford them and the room slowly became fully furnished. Artwork by different members as well as posters with positive messages began appearing on the walls as additional members were steadily added to the group. One of the favorite things for Adam was the stage. There were no planned programs, but different members with a variety of talents would go to the stage at their own time and pace and perform. Some people were individual artists while others formed into bands, choirs, and quartets with a variety of music. So on a given night you might hear instrumental music from a combo or you might hear Christian rock being belted out by a singer backed by drums, guitars, bass and keyboard. A choir sometimes sang, either a cappella or sometimes accompanied by recorded music. There was even a barbershop quartet that harmonized old hymns two or three times each month. One of Adam's favorites was a man named Seymour who was a poet. He occasionally shared poems they had heard before, but usually he offered one that he had just composed. One of the members had suggested that after one of his poems, they should all snap their fingers like in the old beatnik coffee shops and so now everyone snapped as loudly as they could when he finished. It never failed to bring a good-natured laugh.

Of course one of the primary benefits was simply sitting around the tables. Transparency was highly encouraged and people would share their burdens, their regrets, their fears, whatever was on their mind at the time and others at the table gave them support. Support could come in the form of simple encouragement, but it could also be suggestions, ideas, and prayers. As wonderful as the atmosphere and the performances were, this was what people needed the most.

Membership increased little by little and someday they would have to expand or start a second location. That was a problem that Adam looked forward to addressing, but for now his concern was only one thing: finding Paula.

He continued canvassing downtown, going up one side of a street and down the other side. He knew the downtown area well enough that he was doing a grid search, working one street then any adjoining alleyways and on to the next street. It was a long and tedious process but it was what was needed to find someone like Paula. He thought about enlisting help from the members and he knew they would eagerly join him, but they were at the club for their own needs and reasons and he didn't like to distract them from that. James was more than willing to help but he was the one person that Adam could depend on to be at the club and serve as a leader when he couldn't be there himself. So he took it upon himself to be the search party.

He turned up an alley off of 10th street and saw the legs of somebody stretched out with their back against the brick wall of a building. A short skirt was wrapped around the upper portion of the legs which were bare below the knees. It was definitely a woman and Adam's heart surged as he approached, thinking that this might be Paula. But as he drew near he saw that it was another woman, one ten or twelve years older than Paula and someone who had definitely had a rough life. She looked up and took a cigarette from her mouth as he approached and said "Bless you sir, could you help a poor soul with money for some food"?

He looked her in the eyes and said "You say bless me. Do you believe in God, sister? Do you know him?"

"Oh yes sir I do" she replied.

"Now look me in the eye and tell me that".

"Well, I used to know him sir. When I was a little girl my momma took me to church and all. I even invited him into my life and got baptized when I was like eleven. I guess I don't know him now like I did then."

Adam then asked her name, which was Sarah and he said, "Sarah do you know God still loves you? You may have strayed from him, but he has never left you."

"Oh, he's probably through with me. I've done a lot he wouldn't like."

"Doesn't matter. He's there if you really want to turn things around and be with him again. He can give you purpose and a better life." He handed her a card and said, "If you really want that, go the address on that card and ask for James. There will be food there too. I have to go now but you go see James."

"Thank you sir, I will. I promise."

Watching him walk away, Sarah thought to herself "Wow that guy was different. Something about him makes me believe what he says. It's like he's real, not some fake."

He walked on down the alley and then looked back. Sarah was picking up her things and preparing to go. He prayed she would make it to James.

He had now completed his grid search of downtown and no Paula. She might have gone to another area but she had always stayed in this one. As he thought about it, he decided where he would go next. Part of him didn't want to find her there, but the other part just wanted to find her regardless of the location.

## Chapter Six

Tashara walked into the club that afternoon and surveyed the room. There were very few people there, which didn't surprise her given that it was 2:00 PM, the middle of the afternoon. She herself usually came in the evening and stayed until about 9:30 or 10:00, but she had gotten off work early that day and wanted some company instead of crashing at her studio apartment. Mostly out of habit she first went to the coffee bar that had been set up in one corner and was surprised to find a pot that seemed freshly brewed. She hardly noticed the recorded music playing softly in the background as she grabbed a cup and then looked over the room again. This time she spied a lady sitting at a table near the back wall by herself. She appeared to be maybe five or so years older than Tashara and she didn't remember ever meeting her before.

When she approached the table the woman looked up and smiled. Tashara could see now that she had ash blonde hair and wore little makeup. Though she was sitting Tashara could see that she was just a little heavy for her height and she wore jeans and a white cotton blouse. Tashara introduced herself and said, "Mind if I sit?" The lady motioned for her to sit and replied "Of course, please do. I'm Susan by the way". After Tashara got settled Susan looked at her and said, "I don't recall seeing you before. Are you new to the club?"

"No, I just usually come later in the evening after work and dinner. But I got off work early today and decided to drop by. Do you come often in the afternoon?"

"Three or four times a week usually. I come after lunch and leave to pick my son up from middle school about 4:00. He has band practice after his regular classes. It must be nice to get off work early."

Tashara smiled and laughed lightly. "It would be except that it's due to our business slowing down. Management decided this week to start reducing our hours. If it doesn't pick up fairly soon, I'll be looking for part-time work so I can keep the rent paid."

"Oh gosh, I'm so sorry to hear that. If it's okay with you, I'll add you to my prayer list."

"Oh Susan, please do. I would greatly appreciate it."

They both sat then for a while, each lost in their own thoughts. Even though they had just met, it was that comfortable kind of silence that can exist between close friends who don't have to force a conversation. Finally Tashara broke the silence, "So Susan what brings you to the club so often?"

"Oh nothing too dramatic I'm afraid, nothing like some of the stories I've heard from others." Susan then told her story. She had a nice life, living in the suburbs with a caring husband who provided them with a nice home and everything they needed. They had the one child and he was a good kid who did well in school and seemed to be well adjusted. She did mention that with the teen years getting started, she was a little concerned about his future, the friends he might choose and all the concerns that go with parenting a teen these days.

She then shared that despite being so blessed in her life she was alone most of the time, and now even more so with the son getting older and doing more on his own. Her neighbors were nice enough but she wasn't terribly close to any of them. She attended church on Sundays with her family and loved the worship service, but that was only once a week. She had attended a ladies' bible study during the week and while it was educational, she didn't find someone she really clicked with there. So basically she was just lonely and found very little purpose in her life.

"I really was beginning to think something was wrong with me, that I just didn't mix well with other people. That I was just meant to be that way. But then I met Adam. My husband decided that we needed to add a movie room to our house and he hired a local construction company to do the work. Adam was part of that crew and of course he was very nice. You know Adam. On the last day of the project he approached me as they were all leaving and thanked me for providing them lemonade and snacks each afternoon. It was just something I thought would be a nice break for them. He then said 'Susan, if it's not being too personal it just seems to me that you are not a happy person. It seems like you're missing something'. I stumbled through some words to the effect that I was okay and thanked him for being concerned. He then gave me a card with the address for the club and invited me to visit. I would normally have just thrown it away but you know Adam. There was something so genuine and caring about how he spoke with me that I kept it. A week or two later I thought one day: *why not try it.* I did and I just liked the atmosphere. I'm sure it's busier in the evenings but I meet people like you almost every time. I started keeping a prayer book and praying about whatever concerns they may have and many have come back and told me about answered prayers. It just seems that this is my place and I've really felt good here."

Tashara looked at her and said, "Wow that may seem like a simple story to you, but I think it's pretty special."

She then shared her own story. Tashara had been raised in a small town several miles west of the city. She had been the only African American student in her school; actually she was the only minority of any kind in her school and the other students had bullied her from the first grade on up through high school. In elementary school they all acted like they were afraid to touch her because the "blackness" might rub off on them. The teachers had tried to stop their behavior but to no avail. Then in junior high and high school they started calling her derogatory and insulting names. Everyone was afraid to befriend her in any way, fearing the social blow back if they were seen talking or being with her. Up through about the 6th or 7th grade, she went home crying every day, but then in the later years she replaced that with her own hatred of her fellow students. Her preferred method of expression was too outperform them at every opportunity. She graduated valedictorian of her class, showing them that she was smarter than all of them. She was on the girls track team and broke the school record for the 100 and 200 meter dashes. Nothing she did won her any friends, but she took satisfaction in showing them her superiority whenever possible and in whatever way possible.

Upon graduation she moved to the city and went to community college, earning an Associate's Degree in Accounting. "You know Susan, I probably could have made some friends there at the community college. But by then my emotional scars ran very deep. They had made me a different person. Honestly I didn't even like myself sometimes. But then I met Adam, at the grocery store of all places."

She then explained how she was shopping one Saturday and Adam was shopping for groceries at the same store. She kept running into him as she went up one aisle and he was coming down it at the same time. He just smiled at her the first time, and then said something like 'I guess we're on the same path' the next time. They both couldn't help but laugh and then they giggled again when she pulled up with her cart behind him in the checkout line. He finished checking out and left. When she paid and exited she saw that he had just finished putting the groceries in his car, which was parked right next to hers. This was just too much. He grinned as she approached and said, "Well we've been together so far, I might as well help you unload."

Tashara said she would normally have said no thanks, but he seemed so nice and he started helping so quickly she didn't have time to object anyway. When the car was loaded he introduced himself and she replied with her name. He then gave her a card for the club and said he thought she might enjoy it.

"Normally I would have thought he was hitting on me, but like you said earlier it was Adam and he just seemed so different. I put the card in the cup holder of the car and for the next several days I kept seeing it whenever I got in the car. Then I finally thought I would just go by and see what it was like. It wasn't like my social life was preventing me from going there. When I arrived James greeted me and introduced me to some people and then Adam walked in. I went over to him and asked if he remembered me, which of course he did. We sat down and started talking and before I knew it I was sharing my story with him. I couldn't believe I was doing it, but he was so easy to talk with. He told me that God created us all in different colors and thought we were all beautiful. I remember he said 'You know despite all the paintings you see, there's no reason to think Jesus was white'. I had never thought about that and somehow it resonated with me. Well then I started coming more often and now here we are."

They both agreed that it had made a big difference in their lives and then they settled again into a comfortable silence until Susan left to pick her son up from band practice.

## Chapter Seven

Paula sat up against the brick wall of the bus terminal. She had no intention of catching a bus, no matter how appealing getting as far away as possible might be to her. It was simply the first building she had spotted after reaching the south side where other homeless people had congregated. It had taken her all day to walk from downtown to here. No one had seemed eager to give a lift to a women carrying a bag and walking along the thoroughfare that she had traversed. She was understandably exhausted by the time she saw the terminal building. She sat there catching her breath and looked around at the other people lined up along the wall. Most of them looked dirtier, more unkempt and ragged than she did, but she had no doubt she would be in the same shape soon if she couldn't get some money somehow.

A black man sitting to her left who seemed about twice her age looked her over and said, "New around here ain't you?"

"Yeah, I've been hanging in downtown. Had to get out of there."

"Cops?"

"No, just had to get away from some people."

"Been there" he said and then added that his name was Ben.

He asked how long she had been on the street and she answered him with as little detail as possible. She wasn't ready to share her life story with Ben. He then told her about a shelter about five blocks away. The shelter was pretty limited on beds but they did have food and you could get a decent meal there, soup and cornbread a lot of times he said but it was hot and filled you up. It was already shut down for the night, but she thanked him and said she would find it tomorrow. He then asked if she had any weed on her and when she said no, he shuffled down to another spot and struck up a conversation with someone else.

She was glad to learn about the shelter and the food. She would definitely try that, but she really wanted to avoid sleeping in a place like that if possible. She needed a way to pay for a room, even if it was the cheapest place in town. It became dark after a while and she knew she was stuck there for the night. Then another woman sat down in Ben's spot and wrapped herself in a ratty blanket. Like Ben she asked if Paula was new and Paula explained her arrival in the south side. This woman was named Evie and she turned out to be quite a talker. When Paula asked if she knew a way to make a few bucks, Evie said, "You young and not bad lookin'. You shouldn't have a problem. Most girls work the next two or three streets over." Paula said that was good to know but did Evie know any other way and she then shared about a pawn broker who owned a shop just a little farther south of the bus station. "Freddy, he gives you something for clothes, costume jewelry, shoes, stuff like that. But nothing real fancy, he don't want no trouble with the law." Paula quickly picked up that Evie was talking about shop lifted items and asked what stores in the area were good targets. Talkative Evie shared a few ideas with her and then leaned her head back against the brick wall and was soon asleep. Paula, on the other hand, tried to rest but slept very little that night. She hated not having four walls around her.

The next day she took her bag and started walking through her new neighborhood. She located two of the stores that Evie had mentioned and scoped them out. She then went to a nearby convenience store and quietly made her way to the ladies restroom where she washed her face and arms, scrubbing them as best she could with paper towels. She wanted to look like she belonged in these shops and not like the homeless vagrant she now was. Next she found an alleyway close by and stashed her duffel bag there, hoping no one would see and take it before she returned. She took a large canvas bag from the duffel and walked off toward the first store.

The shop was a clothing store. Their merchandise was not high end but more for middle income folks, nice but not luxurious. She looked through some pants and tops and told the saleslady she was just browsing. She waited for the lady to get occupied with another customer and then quietly turned her back and stuffed a pair of pants and a top into the canvas bag and made her way out of the shop. After depositing these items in her duffel bag, she hit the second store where she scored a nice fake pearl necklace and just as fake diamond bracelet. She then went to the pawn shop which turned out to be half a mile away. She told Freddy that Evie had told her about him and she had some stuff to pawn.

Freddy looked at what she had and said, "Okay, seven bucks for all of it."

"Ah, come on Freddy. Ten anyway."

"Eight tops, take it or leave it."

"Alright, I'll take it then."

"And next time take the price tags off the stuff" Freddy said as she walked out.

Adam looked up at the large multi-story municipal building and sighed as he prepared to go in. He still had mixed feelings as he entered the county jail. Part of him hoped Paula was not there, but the other part just wanted to find her no matter where. He walked up toward the front desk behind three other people. Two of these were bondsmen posting bail for inmates and the third was an attorney who explained that he was there to see his client. Adam looked around at the benches that lined the walls of the reception area. These were populated by various people who were obviously family members of the incarcerated. Some were resolute and appeared to have been through this routine before. Others were visibly upset. He was especially struck by an older woman who had tears running down her eyes and he wondered if she was there for a child, or maybe a grandchild.

It was finally his turn at the desk and he approached the man behind the counter. "Hello, Vincent. How are you today?"

"Ah, Brother Adam. I'm doing well. Haven't seen you here in a while. Are you dealing with a nicer crowd nowadays?"

"I don't know. I just take them as the Lord gives them my friend. I'm wondering if you have a young lady named Paula staying with you."

"Doesn't ring a bell but let me check. We did pick up half a dozen or so street walkers last night."

Vincent checked his computer and reported that no Paula was among his current residents. Adam then explained who Paula was and how she had disappeared. He had dealt with Vincent before and had found him generally supportive of Adam's efforts even as he remained a little skeptical about his mission.

"Well, I don't know. These last night came from the downtown area. If your Paula doesn't want to be found she may have just left town. If not that, she might have moved to another area and I would check the south side first. That seems most likely from what you're telling me"

"She's a downtown girl but you may be right. I'll give that a try. Thanks Vincent."

"Good hunting, Adam."

With that Adam walked to his car in a nearby parking lot and thought about what Vincent had suggested. He doubted she had left town and if she had, he had no idea where she would go. Perhaps her parents would know.

He then started his engine, buckled his seat belt and started the drive to the south side.

## Chapter Eight

"Hey dude, fancy seeing you here again tonight" Eric chimed as he walked up to the table where Jacob was sitting.

"Eric, good to see you too young man!" echoed Jacob.

Eric could see that Jacob had been reading his bible. "Sorry, didn't mean to interrupt you there."

"No I was nearly finished. It was just a little online daily devotional I do with some other guys. It normally takes about five minutes a day. I usually do it during lunch but missed it today. I'm caught up now though."

They exchanged a few more pleasantries and then sat quietly listening to a jazz combo on stage that some of the guys had formed. The saxophone player was especially good as he played Cannonball Adderly's Autumn Leaves. When they took a break Jacob said "I'm not normally a big jazz fan but I have to admit that was really good."

"Yeah my old man loved jazz. It's about the only good thing I inherited from him."

"You two didn't get along?"

"No, we definitely did not. Didn't really come here tonight expecting to talk about him, but maybe this is a good time to share my story with someone. Maybe it will be good. We both agreed the other night that we that we each had our own baggage."

He then proceeded to tell Jacob about his earlier life. He had been raised by his parents and his mom was still alive and he loved her very much. His dad had died several years ago when Eric was a senior in high school. He had been an abusive father and husband and Eric's mom had endured the worst of it. His dad constantly subjected her to verbal abuse, telling her she was worthless, that his biggest mistake was marrying her, that she was nothing but garbage, calling her every foul name in the book. To make matters worse he drank heavily and when he was drunk he would resort not just to verbal but also to physical abuse. Many times Eric would find his mom in her room crying with new bruises on face or her arms and shoulders.

But Eric was not immune to his abuse either. He couldn't count the times his father had told him he wished Eric had never been born, that he was nothing but a disappointment and raising him was a burden he shouldn't have to bear. Night after night he told Eric how stupid he was as Eric tried to focus on his homework. He didn't hit Eric as often but there were times when he would slap him in the face with the back of his hand or take a belt to him with far too much enthusiasm. Once a teacher had seen a bruise on Eric's face and asked him about it. He wanted to tell her the truth but he feared that his father's retribution would fall on his mother if he said anything, so he lied and told her he got hit by a baseball that he misplayed during a game.

His father did most of his drinking at home but one night he went out to a bar with some co-workers and crashed his car into a telephone pole on the way home. He died that night in the hospital. Eric never understood why his mother was there at his bedside holding his hand and weeping as he took his last breaths. As much as he hated to admit it, he saw the man's death as a blessing and a new lease on life.

His mother got a job at a local grocery store after the funeral and Eric was fortunate enough to get a college scholarship. He was a pretty good baseball player and got a full-ride at the state college not far from his hometown. While attending school he met his future wife Amanda and they were married soon after graduation. He thought that life had finally turned around for him and it would all be a bed of roses for the two of them. But then something happened that he would never have predicted. He started drinking in the evening after work and worse than that, he started taking his frustrations out by yelling at and demeaning Amanda. Then one night he slapped her hard when she yelled back at him. He slumped to the floor and started crying. Who was he? And why was he acting this way?

He had told Amanda all about his father and the abuse he had undergone. He had told her how much he hated him and never wanted to be like him. Yet here they were. After slapping her that night he promised to change, but three nights later he erupted into another tirade. This time after things quietened down she came to him with her iPhone and said "I want you to listen to this". She had recorded the whole thing. He listened, transfixed by what he heard. When it was over she said "Tell me. Who does that sound like to you?" Memories of his father flooded through him and he agreed that night to go to marriage counseling with her. They had attended a nearby church a few times and now they enrolled in a counseling program there. Most of the sessions were together but there were a few that were scheduled just for the husband or just for the wife. One night after he walked out of one of these one-on-one sessions he saw someone standing near the exit door. It was Adam.

"I don't know why he was there, but he spoke to me and asked how things were going. A perfect stranger but for some reason I unloaded on him and shared everything that was going on in my life. He listened and said the counseling would help and that he would pray for Amanda and me also. Then he gave me a card and invited me to the club. A few nights later some guys from work invited me to have a drink with them that evening. I declined and decided to go try the club out instead. The rest, as they say, is history."

"Wow! How great is that!"

"Okay Jacob, your turn. What got you here?"

"I guess it's only fair to tell you, huh."

With that Jacob began sharing his own story.

Jacob had been raised in church.  In fact his father was the pastor of his church and his mother was very active in the church as well.  Jacob's older brother was a pastor too and so when it came time for college, Jacob began studying for the ministry.  After all he was a believer and it ran in the family.  It just seemed like the thing to do and more than that, he did truly feel that God was calling him to a life of service.  After college he attended a well-known seminary where his bible knowledge grew and where he learned how to deliver a message effectively.  After graduation he became the youth pastor at a church that was two states away from his father and brother's churches.  He wanted to find success on his own and not because one of them helped pave the way for him.

He did well as a youth pastor and really enjoyed working with the kids, building and improving their spiritual lives and preparing them for adulthood.  They had camps and ski trips and mission trips and all sorts of activities and he thoroughly enjoyed it all.  Mostly though he relished seeing them accept God's grace and forgiveness in their lives as their knowledge grew.  He met his wife Sylvie at that first church and they were married after a year-long courtship.  Soon after that he accepted a position at another church where he would be associate pastor and would be working more with the adults.  Three years at this church and then he finally got his own church where he would be lead pastor.  Life seemed to be going well and he and Sylvie were blessed with their first child just after moving to this new church.

There's always a honeymoon period when starting at a new church.  The congregation is glad to welcome you and they are encouraged by the new voice you bring to the worship time.  You in turn are happy to see new faces and are excited about the opportunities you see for the future.  This was the case for that first year but then several things hit in rapid succession that delivered punishing blows to Jacob's outlook.  First their child contracted COVID-19 and then RSV and died before seeing his second birthday.  Jacob and Sylvie, along with the church, had prayed so earnestly for healing.  Why had this happened?  They comforted each other with the knowledge that the sweet baby was in heaven, but the pain was still almost more than they could bear.

Another year went by and though his heart continued to be heavy, Jacob carried on and served with as much enthusiasm as he could muster. Then his brother called one night and told him that their father had been diagnosed with cancer and the doctors had told them it was terminal. Jacob rushed home to see his father and it was almost unbearable to see the man in so much pain. He and his brother prayed fervently that the pain would subside and that God would perform a miracle, but nothing seemed to change. Over the next three months he made many trips home and each just added to his disappointment. When his father succumbed to the disease it was both a tragedy and a blessing. The pain was gone but so was his father.

The church should have been the primary source of comfort for Jacob at this time but instead it just added to his anguish and depression. Some of the church members felt that his messages had become stale and the church was not growing as it should. They even stated that he had spent too much time away from the pulpit and they needed for him to be more dependable. Two of the church leaders came to him and suggested that a change might be best for both him and the church.

Jacob fell into an understandable depression dealing with and hearing this. He began to doubt that he should ever have even entered the ministry. Maybe it had been a mistake all along. And why had all these things happened to him anyway? He felt like he had been loyal to God, but God had abandoned him. God had ignored his pleas for his son and for his father. God had allowed this strife that had now arisen in his church. What had he done to deserve this? He talked with Sylvie and determined that he would give his last message the following Sunday. It was time to leave and do something else.

He delivered that message and people greeted him afterward with hugs and well wishes and promises for prayer.

You would have never guessed their true feelings if you were observing this spectacle. When the last members had left, he turned to go to his office and saw a stranger standing in the hallway. What a day for a visitor! The man came and shook his hand and introduced himself simply as Adam. He then said something so simple and yet so profound to Jacob: "God is not through with you yet. You have important work ahead." He then told Jacob about the club and invited him to visit it. Jacob was very skeptical but there was something about this stranger that intrigued him.

He shared the encounter with Sylvie and she encouraged him to go. "You need something in your life now. Maybe this is it. Try it once and see."

He did and on his first visit Adam met him and they talked for the entire evening. Adam seemed to understand all that was plaguing Jacob and the toll it had on him. But he also saw light at the end of the tunnel and a bright future. He suggested that Jacob seek counselling with a man that he recommended and Jacob followed up on that.

"I went to the counselling and to the club for the next year and then I found a position that I really feel God had in mind for me. I've been there two years now and it's been very fulfilling."

"Where's that?"

"I'm the chaplain for the county jail system and also for the state prison just south of here. Guys that are in the worst positions of their lives but I think I help and give them hope."

"Wow, now that is a story. That's incredible, man!"

Jacob laughed. "Well like we said the other night, we all certainly have our baggage but thanks to the club we all have our redemption too."

"Amen, my friend. Amen."

The jazz combo returned to the stage about that time and began another set.

# Chapter Nine

Adam was beginning to have doubts about the decision to search this new area of the city. He had used the same approach as he used downtown, going street by street and alleyway by alleyway. This was one of the oldest neighborhoods in the city with block after block of tarnished red brick buildings, many with shops and cafes at street level and offices or apartments on the upper floors. He was not nearly as familiar with this area but that didn't really matter as long as he covered it thoroughly. So far he had not seen Paula and no one he questioned could remember anyone matching her description. He had made a mental note that it would be helpful in the future to have a photo of each member to assist in searches like this. As he covered the area he eventually came to the bus depot and saw several homeless people lining the walls of the building and the surrounding grounds.

He asked several people about her but again no one remembered anyone like her, or if they did they didn't trust a stranger enough to share it. Being homeless made you part of an exiled community and they were often reluctant to cooperate with outsiders. Finally he approached an old black man and introduced himself. The man responded and said his name was Ben. Adam felt a glimmer of hope when Ben said that yes he remembered a young girl matching that description. He had told her about a nearby shelter where she could get a meal and a cot for the night. He didn't know if she had gone there or not.

"She didn't seem like she had been on the street too long. I hope she's alright," Ben said as Adam thanked him and moved on to question others. That turned out to be fruitless however. No one else that he spoke to recalled such a person.

The sun had just started to set while he was talking to Ben, and Adam decided that he would check with the shelter before deciding his next move. The shelter was a large room with long picnic style tables and they were serving dinner when he arrived. Dinner tonight consisted of a beefy vegetable soup, corn bread and tea or coffee to drink. He asked one of the servers who was in charge and was pointed to a thin gray-haired lady who had a quick smile and pronounced crow's feet at the corner of each eye. He went over and introduced himself and she smiled and shook his hand. "Thelma" was all she said. He explained who he was looking for and Thelma told him that she did remember such a girl and in fact her name had been Paula. She had come in a couple of times for meals but had never stayed the night. However she had not seen her in the last few days.

Adam walked out of the shelter and thought about what Thelma had said. If she hadn't been there for food it meant she had left the area, which seemed unlikely, or she had made some money somehow. He knew how Paula had made money in the past. Looking up at the night sky, he now walked toward his car which he had parallel parked at a meter about three blocks away.

Paula stood near the jewelry area of the department store. She had been in this store twice in the past week, each time lifting a small amount of jewelry or clothing and selling it to Freddy. Maybe it was just her imagination, but this time she felt like one of the salesladies was watching her very closely, too closely. Were they on to her? Maybe or maybe not but when the lady started walking her way, she starting walking toward the exit.

The lady crossed an aisle and cut her off asking "Is there something I can help you with?"

"Oh no, I was just browsing".

"Well let me know if I can help you find anything".

She thanked the woman and made her exit from the store. She was sure that they remembered seeing her before. There were just not enough nice stores in this area to keep shoplifting. Eventually she would get caught, and besides that Freddy didn't pay that much anyhow. She had to find some other way to make money. Her stomach growled at that moment as if to remind her that it needed attention. *What could she do?* She knew the answer to that all too well but she now concluded that she might not have another choice. A tear rolled down each cheek as she acknowledged this grim reality. *This was never what I wanted. Why did that man have to come in the restaurant and recognize me?*

She began walking away from the store, each step filled with reluctance. She pictured herself walking with a giant heavy iron anchor tied to her neck, and indeed that was how she felt as she walked toward this new chapter in her life. Thirty five minutes later she was on a street that housed several bars on the ground level of the red brick buildings. She looked up the street and saw girls standing at various spots along the street. As men passed slowly down the street in their cars the girls would walk up to them and greet them. Some of the girls got in cars with the men they approached, while others walked back to the sidewalk ready to approach the next car. She knew how the game was played and walked up the street looking for a spot of her own. She finally found one that seemed unoccupied and the girls several yards away on either side of her didn't seem to mind. She looked up at the sky and drew a deep breath, reconciling herself to what she had to do.

She watched the first couple of cars pass by and then as the next one approached, she decided to get it over with and walked up to the car. She couldn't look the driver in the eye and was looking over the roof of the car as the man rolled down his window and she said "Hey Mr. looking for a good time tonight?"

"No" said the man. "I'm looking for you. Hop in." She knew that voice. Imagine her shock when she looked down at the window and saw Adam in the car.

"Oh Adam! No! No! No! What are you doing here?"

"Get in. Let's talk"

She slowly went around the front of the car and opened the passenger door and took a seat. She had never wanted Adam to see her like this. Tears now gushed down her cheeks. Adam drove to a quieter street and parked the car. He turned to her and said "I've been looking everywhere for you. I'm so glad I finally found you."

"You weren't supposed to find me. Adam, just go away. You're a good person, but I'm a lost cause. I'm a loser and I've disappointed you and everyone else at the club. Please just go away."

"You haven't disappointed anyone, Paula. And no, you're not a loser. You're a precious child of God. He still loves you and so do we."

They then talked for several minutes. She explained what had happened at the restaurant and why she had left. Adam told her that he understood, but that she had to know that there was always a risk that people from her past would recognize her. He said that when they did the only thing to do was to own it and tell them how God had forgiven her and changed her life. Actually it might even turn out to be a good thing because her testimony might change the life of that person who recognized her. She understood this, but it was still hard to accept. But she slowly came to see that Adam and the others were there to support her, to build her up and not to tear her down.

She finally agreed to go back to the club with him, but she said there was one thing that she wanted him to know first. "Adam, you were the first man I approached. I haven't sold myself before. I did sleep with one guy and I shoplifted and I know that's just as wrong but I haven't done the other."

He believed her and told her so. "Now before we go to the club I want us to make one other stop on the way."

He then told her about meeting her parents and how worried they were and how much they still loved her.

She was very ashamed and afraid to meet them but she reluctantly said, "Okay, I'll go if you go in with me."

"Of course."

The visit was short. Her parents were overjoyed to see her. Both of them cried and hugged her for what seemed like forever. They thanked Adam for finding her and hugged him too. Paula was shy at first but quickly warmed up and promised them that she was a new Paula and they would see her more often.

When they got back in the car Paula thanked him for taking her there. "It was the right thing to do. They really do still love me. I can hardly believe it."

"Yes they do. And now on to the club."

## Chapter Ten

It was Saturday night and the club was busy. It was always busy on Friday and Saturday nights. Many members simply chose the club as a safe alternative to places they had gone in the past on weekends. Others had no other plans for the evening and chose the fellowship of the club over a lonely evening at home. Everyone had their reasons, but this particular Saturday seemed even busier than usual. A band was on stage playing Christian rock and many were singing along with the familiar songs, while others sat at the tables and talked above the noise. Everyone was a little surprised when James took the stage after the band ended a popular song and took the microphone from the singer.

"Listen up, everyone" he began. "I've got exciting news. Several of you have asked and I just wanted to let you know that I heard from Adam a few minutes ago. He has found Paula and they should be here in about twenty minutes. As you know people come and go here as they please, but I have a special request tonight. If you look around and don't see an acquaintance here tonight, try giving them a call or text them and tell them the good news. We want to celebrate Paula's return to us and they may want to join us for that."

Everyone burst into applause at this welcome news and you could see several looking around the room and others already on their phones. This was indeed a cause for joy. The band began to play a praise song and almost everyone joined in and started singing at the top of their lungs. Soon a few others started coming in and joined in the singing as the crowd grew.

Adam and Paula continued to talk after they left her parents. This had been an ordeal for her and although she felt relieved that Adam had found her, she still had several concerns and her confidence definitely needed a boost. Adam continued to reassure her that the others would welcome her with open arms and that she was not the first who had strayed and later returned to the group.

He knew that she was also hungry and, while there was food at the club, everyone would be so anxious to greet her and speak with her that eating would not be easy. So he pulled in at a drive-in fast food place and asked her what she would like.

"Ooh, I'm so hungry. I haven't had a cheeseburger since I don't know when. Can I have a cheeseburger and some French fries? "

"Of course and what to drink?"

He ordered both of them a milkshake, strawberry for her and peanut butter flavored for him. They sat and talked more until the food arrived. Paula started gulping down the burger and he reminded her to slow down, eating that fast might make her sick with her stomach so empty. She made a conscious effort to do that and after finishing the burger she started attacking the fries.

When her appetite was sated Paula had another serious thought and said, "Well I'm not hungry for the time being, but where does my next meal come from? I'm sure that the restaurant won't take me back."

"Don't worry. We'll find you something. James and I know some people and so do others at the club."

"I hope so. I really need the work. You sound pretty sure."

Adam now laughed lightly and said, "Well not long ago I found a job for a guy on his first day out of prison. I'm sure we can find you something too."

When they had slurped the last of their shakes, he started the engine and they drove once again toward the club. They were now only about ten minutes away.

"Do you think there will be a lot of people tonight?" she asked.

"You know, I just have a feeling that there will be" he responded.

Shortly after that they pulled into a parking space about half a block from the club and walked the final distance. When they first entered the room people were singing and didn't notice them, but then a few people looked their way and started clapping loudly. Others quickly picked up on this and looked at them and started clapping just as loudly until eventually the music had stopped and the singing grew silent as everyone clapped and whistled and shouted praises. Adam held Paula's hand and they made their way toward the stage with people stopping them along the way and telling Paula how glad they were to see her. Shy at first and perhaps still a little ashamed, Paula's demeanor gradually transformed to one of pure delight.

She and Adam took the stage and Adam addressed the crowd. "I know everyone has been praying for this and I'm so happy to tell you that Paula has been found and is now rejoining us."

Applause again erupted and then people at one table shouted "We love you, Paula!" Soon everyone in the room was repeating this over and over again. "We love you, Paula! We love you, Paula!" Adam allowed this to go on for several minutes because he knew it renewed Paula's strength and resolve. Then he addressed the crowd for a final time.

"You know it's easy to lose sight of how much God loves us and because of that, how much we love each other. When Paula was gone and struggling, she couldn't see that love and felt alone and defeated. We've all felt that way at times, I know. And yet the one thing we *can* know and always be assured of is his love for us. In the book of Isaiah in chapter 54 and verse 10 we find it written:

*Though the mountains be shaken*
*and the hills be removed,*
*yet my unfailing love for you will not be shaken*
*nor my covenant of peace be removed,*
*says the LORD, who has compassion on you.*

Paula and all the rest of us can cling to that promise in the best and the worst of times."

Roberto was sitting at a table in the back of the room with a new friend. Philip had been coming to the club for a few months but this was the first time they had connected and gotten to know each other. Roberto turned to him now and said, "You know, it's great that Paula is back, but do you know what I think is even greater"?

"What's that?"

"How many people you think are here tonight?"

"Gee, I don't know. Ninety, a hundred, maybe a few more."

"Yeah, and if you or me or anyone here tonight disappeared tomorrow, Adam would be just as determined to find us as he was to find her. He would leave the rest of us to find that one who needed finding".

"No doubt about it. Isn't there something in the Bible about that?"

Roberto considered this and answered, "Sounds about right, amigo. Sounds about right."

## Epilogue

If you weren't quite sure about the parable that inspired this story, the last page may have been the clue you needed. The Rescue is based on and inspired by the parable of the lost sheep. Jesus actually tells this parable on two different occasions to two difference audiences.

In Luke 15:1-7 he is addressing a group of tax collectors and others described as sinners. Also in the audience are Pharisees and Scribes who have on numerous occasions criticized Jesus for associating with people like the tax collectors. Jesus uses the parable to chide the Pharisees and Scribes. In this telling the lost sheep is someone like the tax collectors who is spiritually lost and the shepherd finding the lost sheep is a sign of redemption. He is telling the Scribes and Pharisees that rather than criticize him, they should rejoice that He is teaching these sinners about the Kingdom of God and bringing them into the fold.

In Matthew 18:12-14 Jesus again tells this parable, but this time it is simply to his disciples. In this telling Jesus is teaching his disciples the importance of the church body. Prior to telling the parable he had instructed them that the believer should have a humble and childlike faith, believing unequivocally in God's goodness and mercy. He has also warned them that the world presents believers with many stumbling blocks and they should be on guard against them. Then he relates the parable itself and the message here is that the disciples and all spiritual leaders should be concerned whenever a fellow believer wanders off the path and returns to a life of sin, whether it's due to their own succumbing to temptation or because someone else is causing them to stumble and leading them astray.

The Rescue is based on the parable as told in Matthew. Adam is a spiritual leader or shepherd who is responsible for a group of believers who assemble together for support in their spiritual journey. Paula, a new member of the group, is the lost sheep who has felt the need to return to her former life and Adam is on a mission to find her and return her to the fold. While the others miss Adam, they understand his purpose in going after Paula and know that not only will he return, but he would do the same thing for them if they were in Paula's place.

Here is the parable from Matthew Chapter 18:12-14 in the NIV Translation:

12) *"What do you think? If a man owns a hundred sheep, and one of them wanders away, will he not leave the ninety-nine on the hills and go to look for the one that wandered off?* 13) *And if he finds it, truly I tell you, he is happier about that one sheep than about the ninety-nine that did not wander off.* 14) *In the same way your Father in heaven is not willing that any of these little ones should perish."*

# The
# Testing

*by*
*Bobby J Watson*

*Having the answers is not essential to living. What is essential is the sense of God's presence during dark seasons of questioning.*

**- Ravi Zacharias**

# Chapter One

Nathan Jobe had just attended the opening of his latest restaurant and was preparing to return home. This particular restaurant represented a milestone as it was the 250$^{th}$ in his nationwide chain of fine dining establishments. Nathan had thanked the management team and all the team members for their diligent work that had made this night a success. He had concluded by thanking God for the success that he and his employees had achieved. Success was putting it mildly in Nathan's case because he was indeed a wealthy man and successful according to any criteria used to define it. He was quite probably the wealthiest man in the state and enjoyed a remarkably happy family life with a loving and devoted wife and three happy and beautiful children. Nathan's only regret about today's event was that his youngest child was celebrating a birthday with a catered party at their home, while he was attending this grand opening. He had facetimed with the child but it just wasn't the same as being there.

As he neared the limousine that would take him to his private jet, a local television reporter and a cameraman approached him, but he politely told them he was in a hurry and could take no more questions tonight. They walked backed to their car, anxious to get their report ready for the 10:00 PM newscast. The cameraman said "You know he must be quite a guy. People love working for him and I've never heard anyone make a negative comment about him. I hear that he's even active in his church and does a lot for the community."

Lucas Ferrano, the reporter, replied to this "Well, you know it's easy to be so upstanding when you're on top like him. But if something happened and he lost all that money and the private planes and all that, then he'd fume and cuss and complain just like the rest of us. Strip all that away and you would see that he's nothing special."

"Maybe so. I guess we'll never know for sure. But I'm putting my money on him. I think he's the real deal." replied the cameraman.

Ferrano persisted, "Let me tell you, I've been around this old earth a few times and I promise you that even if he maintained his cool when everything was taken away, he'd really lose it if his family was destroyed or he got some disease himself. I've seen plenty of these holy rollers curse their precious God whenever things go against them."

Nathan sat in the back of the limo and called his wife on her cell phone. He told her that he would be getting home after midnight and then he asked about the party. "The kids had a great time with the bounce house and the magician did a wonderful show for them. It was a birthday party they'll always remember. There are a few still here waiting for their parents to pick them up but most have gone home." They then discussed some school events that were coming up. It was nearing the end of the school year and each child had some type of program or other activity to mark the event. Nathan told his wife again when he expected to be home and they ended the call.

The limo pulled up to a hangar where his private jet was parked. The pilot had been told they were on the way and had filed his flight plan. He had already refueled the aircraft and they were underway twenty minutes after arriving at the hangar. As the plane left the ground Nathan looked down upon the lights of the city below and reflected on his success. He had started with a small café that served breakfast and lunch and now oversaw 250 of the best fine dining restaurants in the country. He knew that he had not done this alone. He had been fortunate to hire excellent managers and staff, each as dedicated as he was to the success of their company. They had watched communities grow and had built their restaurants in locations that helped achieve success. Nathan knew however that the primary ingredient in his recipe for success was that God had chosen to bless him.

Since childhood Nathan had possessed a deep and abiding faith in God. His parents, both now deceased, had instilled this in their only child from an early age. At a time when many celebrities and politicians loudly proclaimed their faith as part of projecting a positive image, Nathan quietly read his Bible, prayed, attended services and helped fund worthy causes. His faith was born from a true adoration of the Creator. He loved the Lord and tried to live in a manner that pleased Him.

As the plane reached its cruising altitude, Nathan started going through emails and reports that needed his attention. An hour or so later he closed his laptop, reclined in his seat, and drifted off to sleep. He was awakened some time later as the plane hit some rough air. Once it smoothed out, he walked up to the cockpit and was informed by the co-pilot that they would be landing in about thirty minutes. He then went back to his seat and buckled the seatbelt. As promised the wheels hit the ground a half hour later. The small airfield was dark and deserted as they touched down and taxied to the hangar that Nathan had purchased for his jet. It still seemed a little strange to own a private plane and fly alone or sometimes with part of the management team. He had flown commercial until about a year ago when he decided that it was simply easier to have a plane that was available whenever he needed it.

The pilot lowered the steps and he walked down them and spotted a set of headlights coming toward them. Nathan loved to drive but he had accepted the fact that in his position it was better to have a chauffeur and a limo. This freed him up to concentrate on business matters and not get distracted. The driver now parked close to the hangar and came and helped Nathan stow away his luggage. A few minutes later they were on their way home and tonight instead of working he just watched the scenery along their route and anticipated seeing his wife and children soon.

Nothing that happened that day, nothing that happened on the flight or on the drive home gave a hint as to what was awaiting him. Nothing that he could have done would have prepared him for what was coming. There was no forewarning of how much his life would soon change.

# Chapter Two

"Did you have a successful trip, Mr. Jobe?" asked the chauffeur as they exited the airport. Nathan smiled and said, "Carl, I've told you before to just call me Nathan. And yes it was a very successful trip."

"Okay, Nathan. It still just seems strange to not call my boss Mr. I guess you're anxious to get home, Nathan?"

"Absolutely, I hate that I missed my daughter's birthday party but sometimes you just have to do what the job requires." They then chatted about the latest sports news. Carl was a big time basketball fan and they covered both professional and college ball before moving on to the latest baseball news. As they arrived in the neighborhood where the Jobes lived, they both noticed that there were limbs and a couple of trees down. "Wow! When I called home earlier my wife didn't mention storms or anything. It must have arrived after the phone call."

They then pulled onto the street where the Jobes lived and drove to the cul-de-sac where the house was located. Two firetrucks, a police car and an ambulance sat in the cul-de-sac with lights flaring. Nathan's heart leaped when he realized what had brought these first responders there. His house was the largest in the area with five bedrooms, four bathrooms, and over 5000 square feet, but what he now saw where the house should have been was just a pile of rubble. Bricks were strewn upon bricks and only one wall was still standing. He got out of the limo and just stood there dumbfounded. Carl came and stood beside him but he too was speechless. A fire chief saw them and came over to where they stood.

"Is this your house, sir?"

Nathan just stood in the same spot transfixed, but nodded his head to indicate yes. Then he spoke in a whisper as if afraid to hear the answer, "My wife, my children"?

"Sir, how many children do you have?"

Nathan still just stood there in shock and Carl told the chief that there were three children. He also told him Nathan's name.

The chief then stood right in front of Nathan obscuring his view of the rubble. He put his hands on Nathan's shoulders and gently shook him until Nathan looked him in the eye. Then he said "Mr. Jobe, there's no good way to tell you this. A tornado touched down here. Your children are all gone sir. They died in the collapse. We just found your wife and they are bringing her out to the ambulance. She's still alive but badly hurt."

Tears now flowed down Nathan's cheeks as the words from the chief sunk in. He then saw two men coming toward them with a stretcher on which lay his wife. He rushed to her before they put her in the ambulance. Her hair was full of dirt and bits of brick and wood. Her face was badly bruised as if she had been in a fist fight. He couldn't see the rest of her body but something told him it was even worse. She saw him approach and cried to him "Nathan, where are the children? Why did this happen to us?" He tried to calm her but she could see the anguish on his face and knew that they were gone. He finally spoke, "I'll meet you at the hospital. You won't be alone."

Before they closed the ambulance door she looked at him again and said, "I heard someone say that ours was the only house destroyed. Why? Why Nathan? Why has God done this to us?"

He had no answer. He just looked at her and shook his head as if to say he didn't understand it either.

Carl had been by his side this whole time and now took him by the arm and said "Come on, Nathan. There's nothing we can do here. I'll take you to the hospital where you can see her again."

It was well past midnight now and there was little to no traffic as Carl transported them to the hospital. They didn't arrive with the ambulance, but they were not far behind. They went to the Emergency Room and Carl talked to the person at the admissions desk to find out where they had taken Ms. Jobe. He then took Nathan by the arm again and they rode an elevator to the third floor where surgery was underway. He settled Nathan into a chair and then went to a vending machine and got coffee for both of them. He didn't know how long their wait would be, but he knew he couldn't leave his employer alone right now.

Nearly two hours later a doctor emerged wearing light blue scrubs and walked toward them. "Which one of you is Mr. Jobe?" he asked. Nathan had recovered enough to indicate that it was him. "Mr. Jobe, sir we did everything we could but your wife had severe internal damage and hemorrhaging and we couldn't save her. I'm so very sorry." Nathan managed to say "Thank you Doc for trying" and then he slumped into the chair and hung his head in his hands. He then starting chanting in ever increasing volume: "No! No! No!" over and over again. Carl sat by him and put his arm around Nathan's shoulder. He had only worked as a chauffeur for six months but he had never had a kinder, more thoughtful employer and he hated seeing him in such despair.

Finally Nathan recovered his composure enough to ask Carl where the chapel was in the hospital. Carl asked an aide at the nurse station who told him it was on the first floor, not far from the ER. They rode the elevator again and exited to the right when the doors opened. Down the hallway from the elevator they found the chapel on the left side of the hall.

Nathan walked in and got on his knees, resting his elbows on a pew and was silent for the first minute or two. Finally he prayed aloud "Father God, I know that I came into the world with nothing and I'll have nothing when I leave it. You gave me this beautiful family. You gave them and you can take them away. But O God, why did this have to happen? Why Lord, why?" He then meditated in silence for several more minutes before standing and telling Carl it was time to leave.

Tomorrow he would go the office and tell his staff this terrible news. They deserved to know. Then he had four funerals to plan.

## Chapter Three

Nathan woke up the next day a little after noon. Carl had taken him to a nearby hotel and they agreed that Nathan would call him when he was awake and ready to attend to details the next day. His sleep had been deep and surprisingly refreshing and it took him a few minutes to realize where he was and also to realize that the events of the previous night were real. It was not a nightmare, but all too real. He got up from bed and showered and then went downstairs to the hotel restaurant where he ordered breakfast even though it was now nearly 1:30 PM. Despite the despair and anguish he felt, he was ravenous and had two eggs over medium, five strips of bacon and three biscuits with gravy accompanied by orange juice and three cups of coffee.

Physically restored now, he called Carl who arrived about fifteen minutes later. He knew this was going to be a most difficult day and that he had to steel himself for it but he resolved to do everything that was needed. The first stop was his office where he told his corporate employees about the deaths of his family and the destruction of his home. Most had already heard the news by now but they quietly and respectfully listened and then several approached him to say that he would be in their prayers and they would do whatever he needed to get through this ordeal. He thanked them and said he would be out of the office for the next few days, which they had already anticipated. Thankfully he had a very good management team who would keep everything running smoothly.

The next stop was his church where he met with the pastor and informed him of everything. The pastor prayed with him and pledged to support him any way that he could. They agreed to meet again to plan funeral details after Nathan had made arrangements. Those arrangements first included a trip to a mortuary where he picked out four caskets. He had never thought what buying a casket entailed. The most difficult part was choosing three child size units for his three children. This was something no parent should ever be forced to do, but here he was comparing different models and trying to choose coffins that somehow related to each child. Things like their favorite color, interior design and so forth had to be weighed and related to each child. Picking out one for his wife was somewhat more straight forward but no easier.

After choosing and paying for the caskets, they determined when the bodies would be ready, and Nathan realized he would have to buy appropriate clothes for each person since nothing had been saved when their house was destroyed. He also called the pastor and asked if the funerals could be held in the church to which the pastor readily gave his assent. Finally, he purchased five burial plots in the nearby cemetery. He and his wife were still so young they had never considered the need for this, but he now purchased plots on a gentle hillside under a large oak tree. It seemed like a serene place and one that he would feel comfortable in since he knew he would visit often.

Carl then drove him back to the hotel, which would be his home for the foreseeable future. He went up to his room and changed into a pair of nice jeans and a polo shirt before going down to the restaurant for dinner. He had a flank steak, mashed potatoes and asparagus spears for dinner along with a couple of dinner rolls and then took the elevator back to his room on the top floor. Once inside he let go of the resolve that had enabled him to do what was needed today and let his emotions take over. Tears ran like rivulets down his cheeks. He sat at the desk in the room and pounded the top of the desk several times with his fist. Finally he spoke to God.

"Father God, thank you for helping me through this day. I am grateful but I'm still confused. Haven't I lived a life dedicated to you? Why did you not protect my wife, my boys, and my little girl? Tell me why O Lord, tell me why."

He crossed his arms and rested his head on the desk and let the tears continue to flow. He stayed in his room the next day and did not call Carl. He continued to weep and ask God to explain why this tragedy had happened. God did not respond.

Nathan had been an only child and had no other close relatives, but his wife had a sister and he called her and told her the terrible news. He assured her that he would let her know the date of the funerals and he would pay for her stay at the hotel.

The funeral took place a couple of days later and was a surreal affair with all four caskets at the front of the church sanctuary. He and the sister were the only family but the church was packed with friends, employees, and business associates. The pastor delivered a nice homily and spoke of the eternal peace they would now have as they spent eternity with God Himself. The procession to the cemetery was long and it took over an hour for everyone to arrive for the burials. Again the pastor spoke for a few minutes and then the caskets were lowered into the ground. Nathan quietly wept as did the sister. Then what seemed like hundreds of people came by to shake their hand or hug them and assure them that they would pray for them.

Finally everyone had left and it was just Nathan and the sister standing for a few final moments at the fresh graves. He told her he would have headstones erected within a few days if she wanted to come back then. She nodded her assent.

Nathan had never known the sister that well, but they had always been cordial to each other. She now spoke and said, "I know you and my sister were God-fearing but all of that meant nothing in the end, did it? For all your worship of God, He let this happen, and your life is meaningless now too. You might as well have died in that house with them."

He was surprised to hear her harsh words and replied, "I know you're hurting. We both are, but that's a very simplistic view of God. I don't understand why this had to happen either, but we can't just accept the blessings from Him. We have to accept the adversity too."

She shook her head indicating she didn't buy that at all and they parted, her back to her home and Nathan to his hotel room.

Lucas Ferrano, the reporter, and his cameraman had sat quietly in the last pew in the large auditorium along with a handful of other media people. Hearing about the tragedy that Nathan Jobe experienced , they had traveled to his home town to cover the funeral. They had followed the procession to the cemetery after the rest of the media had departed and heard the conversation between Jobe and his sister-in-law. The cameraman looked at Lucas and said "You have to admit I was right. This guy is the real deal. I can't imagine anyone holding up so well in these circumstances." The reporter nodded his head slightly but then said, "Yes, it would seem so. He's the kind that will bury himself in work now to block it out. But let's not give him any medals yet. If something happened with his business or even himself now, it would be the straw that broke the camel's back. He would curse God just like that sister-in-law then, I assure you."

## Chapter Four

Nathan forced himself to go through the rubble that had once been his home. It is amazing how destructive a tornado can be. It's also amazing how selective a tornado can seem. The other homes in his neighborhood had some trees and shrubs knocked down. It was a neighborhood where few people parked in the street, but four or five cars had been shoved around and damaged. No other people had been hurt, a blessing that brought Nathan both thanksgiving and chagrin. Why was it only his family? Indeed when looked at objectively the logical conclusion was that his home and his family had been targeted. Although this thought kept creeping into his mind, he refused to let it take up permanent residence.

The degree of destruction was phenomenal. He found nothing that was worth keeping. He had hoped to at least find some pictures or other remembrances of his wife and children. His wife kept scrapbooks full of pictures for each child as well as special occasions and vacations. But he found none of these. A few neighbors saw him and came up and offered their condolences. He appreciated that, but after stumbling around for two hours and finding nothing worth keeping he returned to the hotel. He had something over three hundred pictures on his phone and it seemed that these would serve as his only reminders of better times. He made a mental note to send those in a file to his administrative assistant who would have them printed and put into an album.

He spent the rest of that week in his room, often going through the pictures on his phone and recalling with fondness the good times they represented. Over the weekend he decided that the best thing he could do was return to work. Perhaps if he buried himself in his work it would ease the pain and enable him to focus on something more positive. He would never get over this disaster, but he could learn to live with it.

The first day back in the office made him doubt his decision as almost every employee came by to pay their respects. But as the day wound down the office visits did also and he knew the next day would be better. He left for the hotel about 5:00 PM that evening and when he entered his room, he turned on the television. He didn't watch a lot of TV but he did like to see the news, and besides the noise it produced was his only companion. He found the channel where ABC World News aired with David Muir serving as the anchor. His wife had always liked David. He listened casually as he changed into more comfortable clothes. There were reports about problems in the Middle East and about threats from Russia to invade some country that he had never heard of before. Midway through the program attention turned to domestic news and he was surprised to hear the name of his restaurant.

He sat on the sofa and listened to a report that a number of his restaurants in the Midwest had been identified as the cause of a serious listeria outbreak. Listeriosis is a rare but potentially very deadly food born disease. It had been determined that some people had been served undercooked meat that contained the bacteria and others had contracted it from fruits and vegetables served in salads. So far five people had died and several others had been sick. They were trying to locate everyone who had eaten at one of his restaurants in the last two weeks.

This news was especially shocking not just because it was his restaurants but because he had always insisted on very strict standards of cleanliness and proper cooking to avoid food borne illnesses. How had this happened with all the precautions his restaurant staff took? He slept fitfully that night as this question kept nagging at him.

When he arrived at his office the next morning he called a meeting of his senior management to discuss the situation. As the meeting was just getting underway his Public Relations Director came in and announced that there had been three more deaths during the night. This prompted Nathan to order the immediate closing of every restaurant in that region. Each restaurant was to undergo a deep cleaning and all fruits and vegetables were to be discarded. Every kitchen staff member was to be instructed again in safety measures that should prevent this disease from continuing to spread.

Over the next two days the national and local news gave full attention to this outbreak and twenty seven more people died from listeriosis. The story also took an unexpected turn as cases began to appear at his restaurants in other regions of the country. By the third day every single location had been closed for deep cleaning and training. The number of deaths increased daily and now seventy eight people had died. Along with the terrible news of deaths, lawsuits now began to come in. Not only was the company being sued but Nathan himself was named in several suits.

The following week restaurants began to reopen, but stood mostly empty due to the extensive news coverage scaring people away. The restaurants that bore his name had become anathema. As he looked ahead to the effects this was having on the business, Nathan determined that he would not be able to make payroll after the next couple of weeks so he announced layoffs in most locations and temporary closing of several locations. By the end of the second week the toll of idle restaurants and a growing number of lawsuits forced Nathan to do something he had never thought possible. He worked with his attorneys to file Chapter 11 bankruptcy and closed all locations until further notice. All but the most vital employees were laid off with no promise of a return to work date.

He awoke the morning following the bankruptcy announcement with the feeling that something was crawling on him along with the sensation of being stung or bitten. He jumped out of bed and looked for bed bugs or whatever was causing this but saw nothing. He then noticed scabs and what appeared to be pricks or bite marks on his shoulders. He turned his back to a mirror and saw the same infestation on his back. It would later be determined that he had Morgellons disease. This disease could affect one's concentration and mood. The exact cause was undetermined and some scientists believed it was a mental health problem.

Nathan sat on the bed looking at himself and began to weep. *Why Lord?* He asked himself. He knew that life had its blessings and its problems, ups and downs, but why was he being barraged with all of this at once? *Why Lord?*

## Chapter Five

Nathan stayed in the hotel that day, not wanting his remaining employees to see his condition. The sores on his body itched terribly and he found himself constantly scratching them even though he knew he shouldn't. He was sitting on the sofa with the television off, just lost in his thoughts when he heard a knock on the door to his room. *Who could that be?* He assumed it was one of his staff checking on him or a hotel maid, and started to ignore it. But after the third knock he got up and opened the door. There were four men at the door and the one who had knocked said "Oh, I'm so sorry. I was looking for....oh My God! Nathan, it *is* you. I didn't even recognize you."

The men at the door were his three closest friends in the world: Eli Fox, William "Billy" DaPointe, and Zack Parr. The four of them had been friends virtually all of their lives. They had gone to the same elementary school, junior high and high school. They had played on the high school baseball team together. Nathan was a star pitcher on the team and Zack Parr had been his catcher. Eli Fox was an All-District shortstop, while Billy DaPointe had patrolled center field. Together they had led their team to a state championship their senior year and Nathan had earned a college scholarship to one of the best universities.

The fourth man was younger. His name was Elon Hunt, who had been a freshman when they were seniors. He was a phenom on second base and had helped them win that championship. He had played some minor league ball before an injury had ended his baseball career. Nathan was a little surprised that he would be with the other three since he had not maintained contact with Elon, but he was glad to see him now.

Now as they entered the room you could see the bewilderment as they looked at their friend. They were stunned into silence and finally Billy DaPointe said "My God, Nathan we can't believe what all has happened to you. We want to do whatever we can to help."

Nathan replied simply, "There's nothing to be done."

They then fell into a prolonged silence as they saw that Nathan didn't want to talk about any of his misfortune. The silence lasted for nearly three hours before finally Nathan spoke in a quiet, subdued voice. "I have to tell you guys, I don't understand why all of this has happened but right now I wish I had never been born. It would have been better if I had been aborted or my mother had miscarried. But since I was born, that day should be hated like the old men hated December 7th or like we despise 9/11. I always thought that God blessed the righteous, those who love Him, and afflicted the wicked and the non-believers." He uttered a quiet sarcastic laugh and said "I guess I was obviously wrong about that. I just don't understand."

The four of them listened to Nathan's diatribe and said nothing in response. Knowing of his deep faith they seemed to be at a loss for words until Eli finally spoke up. "Man, no doubt you've been through the wringer. But I know that you have helped several guys when they were down. You've strengthened them and gave them advice and hope. Now it's your turn to be down and you're surprised and impatient about it? Where is your faith now that it's your turn to suffer? You know that man is born for trouble, dude. We bring it on ourselves because we're human. I don't even pretend to be as religious as you are, but I believe that if you repent and turn to God, he'll forgive you and eventually he'll restore you. He can heal your skin, which really stinks by the way, and He can deliver you from all this trouble."

Nathan listened to Eli, his old friend and thought for several minutes before responding. "Bro, you accuse me of being impatient but you see what all has happened to me. Don't I have the right to be impatient given what I've been through? And despite all this I haven't turned against God. You come here and assume that I must be guilty of something or all these things wouldn't have happened to me. I didn't ask you to come. And honestly I don't know right now if God even cares about any of us. If, as you say I need to repent then I ask God what is it I'm to repent of? What great sin have I committed? Why has God suddenly taken this great interest in me and put me in His crosshairs? I just want to understand because right now life seems pretty meaningless to me. I'd just as soon die."

Billy DaPointe was one of those people who are quick to speak, sometimes before they think. To say he was blunt would be a massive understatement and he had held his tongue and listened as long as he could. "Nathan, if you look at how God really deals with people you'd see that He judges them for their wrongdoings. You seem to think you haven't sinned or whatever you want to call it, but God doesn't just randomly attack people. I don't know how you've run your business or what your family life was really like. I always thought you were on the up and up, but what do I know? But I know this: if you were blameless like you want us to believe then you wouldn't be going through all this stuff. God doesn't punish good people."

These words angered Nathan. "What a bunch of hooey, Billy! Look around dude! You know good and well that bad people are not always punished for their wrongdoings. How many times have you seen real scumbags live a great life and die happy? And you've seen really good people suffer for no apparent reason. You know this is true! And if we suffer, what can we do? We can't talk to God. Oh sure, we can pray but we can't really talk to God and ask Him what we've done or why He has acted as He has. There's no lawyer or umpire or anyone who can speak to God for us either. I've thought and thought about what I may have done to offend Him and I come up empty. When you get right down to it, we're just men. God does what He does and right now I wish He would just leave me alone.

Zack Parr was a common sense kind of guy who usually saw things as black or white. "Nathan, you know I'm not as religious as you guys but it seems to me if you achieved all your success because of some kind of godly blessing, then what's happening now must be the other side of the coin. You must have done some things to get the Old Boy pretty mad, maybe even worse than what you've seen so far. If there is a god then he's way above us, dude and you're foolish to try to understand him. Just do like they said and fess up and maybe he'll forgive you."

"Wow! My old catcher speaks. The guy who used to support and work with me like nobody else. And so wise! You guys are a fount of knowledge. I never knew! Don't you think I've seen the same things that you have? Am I not as intelligent as you! I think you're treating this like a sick joke! It's easy to mock and have all the answers when you're not the one suffering. Why even come here if that's all you've got. I wish you'd just be quiet if you've nothing better to say. Don't you think I've asked God over and over what I've done? And I keep coming up with one answer. Nothing! Not Guilty! I would say innocent even if my life depended on it and right now I wish I could just sleep until the day of resurrection."

A prolonged silence once again dominated the room.

# Chapter Six

Nathan knew in his heart that these friends meant well and they were the only ones who had come to check on him. After the silence had lingered for a while, he asked them to eat dinner with him and ordered several dishes from room service. It arrived and Nathan blessed it and they began to eat and talk about the old days. There were even a few bursts of laughter as they remembered the good times. As they wrapped up their meal the mood shifted again as they continued to consider Nathan's condition. Eli was again the first to speak.

"Nathan, my friend, I've held my tongue as the others spoke and as we enjoyed this meal, but I have to be honest with you. What I say, you know I say out of friendship and concern for you. You know that we know just as much about life as you do, but you act like you have some special knowledge. Truth is you sounded like a windbag earlier defending yourself, and our advice seemed to really bother you. The truth is that scoundrels and bad people may succeed for a while but it doesn't last. Any wealth they have doesn't last that long and they fear death more than most. I can't help but think now that perhaps you are one of those."

"Man, you guys are about the worst comforters ever! I could sound holier than thou if I were in your place. But right now I just want a way to appeal my case before God. I know that the righteous ultimately triumph and I am blameless. I *am one of those!*"

Billy DaPointe was incensed to hear Nathan speak this way. "You call us stupid and hold us in contempt when we came to help you? Truth is, looking at you tells me you'll be dead and forgotten soon enough. If you were really so close to God you wouldn't be in this condition." Zack jumped in and shouted "I'll bet if we knew the truth about your business, we'd see that you connived and cheated your way to success. That's why nothing you've done will last past your lifetime."

Nathan responded to these accusations "Why are you guys even here? You've offered no help of any value. I thought you were my friends. I can see that now I'm alone in this world. Even my employees are reluctant to call or look at me. But one thing I do know beyond any doubt: My Redeemer lives and will stand for me in this life or the next one. When I have the opportunity to plead my case before Him, He will see my innocence. Of that I'm sure. There is some reason that He has allowed these things to happen to me, and someday I'll understand. But I can't help but wonder what judgement you fellows might have coming."

Billy countered this by saying "Who the heck do you think you are that you can speak to God? We're no more important to Him than a worm or a maggot."

"Billy, you were a good center fielder, but you're not the brightest bulb in the basket. You're an empty suit, dude. You're right that God is above our ability to describe or understand fully but He hears our prayers and our thoughts. And you guys speak of such wisdom, but true wisdom is simply the fear of God and when we choose to not do or be evil that shows that we have a true understanding of Him. Before all this happened to me, my real happiness was in doing as God would have me do. Simply caring for the poor and dealing fairly with people gave me joy. If I've not been fair and honest then let God judge me, but I believe that I have been upright my whole life."

Elon Hunt had listened to all of this without speaking, perhaps because he was younger or most likely because he wasn't really part of this tight group of friends. "You know I've kept quiet until now because I thought that you guys, being older, would be a little wiser but it's obvious now that you're not. My understanding is that God gives wisdom to those who seek it, and you guys must not have done much seeking. Nathan, I'm just a regular guy like you and I'm not going to try to scare you into repenting. No fire and brimstone, but maybe I can be the one to speak both to you and to God. You say that you are innocent and

God has somehow wrongly judged you. But you know that God is simply greater than man. He is supreme and He cannot judge unjustly. It's not in His character. Listen to me, *you wise men* and perhaps you will learn. God is all-powerful. In a breath He can create everything that is, and in a breath He can end everything that is. There is none like Him and yet you, Nathan, think He should immediately hear your prayer and act upon it. Well let me tell you bud, if your prayer goes unanswered it's because you lack faith and your prayer's empty. I must tell you I hope your ordeal continues until you recant from these accusations you make against Him. Submit to whatever God does to you and give thanks. Then He will restore you."

The room fell silent after Elon spoke. Nathan acknowledged to himself that there was much to think about in what young Elon had said. There was no doubt that God was supreme and Nathan was just one of his creations. If there was a lesson to be learned from his problems, he wanted to learn them.

After a while the others spoke up and things became a bit more cordial. They wished their old friend well and told him they would be praying for his recovery. They spent some more time remembering the old days and laughing about good times they had shared. Elon entertained them with some of the tales from his minor league days. After another hour they left and Nathan had time to himself to digest everything he had thought and heard.

## Chapter Seven

He went to bed soon after they had left but he didn't sleep well. Okay, he hardly slept at all. The pain and itching made it hard to sleep, but this was different as he kept replaying the words of his friends in his mind. Finally he drifted off to sleep, but only for a restless hour or two. Since childhood Nathan had been a person who prayed. He prayed for his family, his business, his church, for friends who needed help of some kind. He now felt an urgent need to pray and got out of bed. Kneeling at bedside he started to pray, but this was different from any prayer he had ever experienced. Instead of saying or thinking words to address God, he was silent. He was waiting for God to speak to him. He waited for some time but then it was as if God was indeed right there speaking to him, and the words frightened him like no prayer ever had.

He heard God ask "Who is this man who would counsel me? Who is this who would instruct me? Who is this great teacher? If you have words for me, then be a man and speak up. Where were you when I created the earth and everything in it? Where were you when I placed the stars and planets in the sky? Where were you when I parted the sea for my people? Did you create the animals that populate the earth? Do you pour rain and snow on the land and command the wind? How could I have done these things without your advice and help?"

Nathan trembled in fear as he heard these words rattle in his head. He answered "Lord, You are truly all-powerful and can do all these things and more. I know that I am as nothing, just an insignificant slug compared to you. I admit that in my anguish and anger, I have questioned and thought things that are beyond my understanding. Hear me now, Lord and instruct me in your way. I repent of all my ill-conceived thoughts and words. Please Lord, forgive and instruct me. I see now that your ways are beyond my comprehension and I can accept these things you allow to happen even if I don't understand them. Knowing that I have your love and fellowship is enough to see me through any situation."

Little did Nathan know that his friend Eli Fox had gone home that same evening and knelt in prayer. He too heard God speak to him in a way he had never experienced. But the message God delivered was much different. "I am not pleased with what you and your friends told my servant Nathan. You told him over and over that his problems were due to sin in his life. You didn't see that sometimes suffering is a test that can purify my children and lead to a truer and fuller righteousness. You came to comfort Nathan and only succeeded in making him feel worse than he did before you came."

Nathan continued his prayer that had turned into a prayer of thanksgiving. He spoke to God and said "I know that my friends meant well. They did what no other friends did: they came to see me, they spent the whole evening here with me and they did try to empathize with my problems, at least at first. I know that their advice was wrong, but I ask that you would forgive them Lord. Even though they upset me, they showed more concern for me than anyone else so again, please forgive them and instruct them as you have me."

He returned to his bed then and slept better than he had in several days. He awoke the next morning and though he still had the sores all over his body, he felt better and could tell that he was on the road to recovery. He called Eli and asked if the friends could come over sometime that day or that evening. Eli said it was Saturday so perhaps everyone was free. He would check and see and he promised they would come as soon as possible. They knocked on his door that afternoon and he welcomed them into his room.

"First I want to thank the four of you for caring and for coming to see me last night. We talked about a lot of things, gosh it was the deepest religious conversation I think I've ever had. I prayed after that and felt closer to God than I ever have."

The friends nodded and said they could tell he felt better already.

"Yes, I do. You know I thought about all that was said and I still do not believe that anything I did caused God to make me lose my family and my health. I'm not perfect, as none of us are, but I didn't commit any sin so grievous that God punished me like that. I don't know why these things all happened but I know that God is supreme and we don't always understand his ways, nor should we expect to understand them. But I did uncover a terrible sin in my life, and I did repent before Him. Guys, I've always hated Bible thumpers who go around quoting scripture and pointing out everyone's sins, but I was guilty of something just as bad. I was a self-righteous jerk. I knew how devoted I was to God and I waved it like the pennant we won when we were state champions. I observed the letter of the Bible but not always the spirit. I was arrogant and self-righteous.

My second sin was questioning God. We can't understand everything God does and we're not supposed to. His plan for our lives is part of a bigger picture and we should not question him. Oh, I don't mean we should never wonder what he's doing or why things happen. Sure, we all do that at times. But if we love and trust him, if we have placed our faith in Jesus then we can know that He means well for us no matter what we are going through at the moment. So we can't question or doubt his motives and his plans for our lives. In my case I wasn't being punished for a particular sin, but I was being tested so that I could be refined and lose my self-righteousness."

Elon Hunt was the first to respond and said "How beautifully put, Nathan. I think we've all learned from this experience." The others nodded in agreement and Eli Fox inserted "I most definitely have." He then shared his own prayer with the group and how God had spoken to him.

"I certainly have too" responded Nathan. "And one more thing I should clear up. I spoke foolishly about having a lawyer or umpire who could speak to God on my behalf. How stupid of me to think that I could stand before God and justify myself to the Creator himself. In my self-righteousness I forgot that we do have that umpire. There is only one who is both God and man, who has experienced what we do and also knows God as no one else does and that of course is our Lord and Savior Jesus Christ."

They continued to talk for the rest of the afternoon, about this experience and then remembering old times. It was a good day.

# Chapter Eight

By Monday Nathan was feeling much better. He still had sores, especially on his neck, torso and hands but they were growing smaller in number each day. He returned to the office and though his remaining employees were shocked at his appearance, they were overjoyed to see him.

After greeting everyone he went into his office and spent the day taking stock of the company's current position. The once proud name of his chain was now a source of embarrassment and even ridicule. His workforce was reduced to those in the corporate office, and even those were only about half what they had been a month ago, plus a handful of district managers in the field. He determined that in order to come out of this disaster, they would have to reemerge as a totally new business with no apparent ties to the old one.

He contacted a consulting group who specialized in the restaurant business and asked for their advice on the best way to do this. He included his own senior management in the discussions and after a week of tossing ideas around they agreed on a plan. It was a bold plan and one that would take some time to execute but it seemed to be the one that offered the best chance of success. They would sell each of their current restaurant locations to competitors and then rebrand under a different name, a different theme and totally new locations. They would be a phoenix rising from the ashes of their old business.

Using a real estate firm that the consultants recommended they began the process of putting the old locations on the market. The competitors who showed an interest were like serpents waiting to strike. They sensed that Nathan and company were in a hopeless situation and tried to buy the locations for a fraction of their value. Nathan knew he would have to discount the price to unload these properties, but he refused to panic and be taken advantage of. The real estate firm was headed by an attractive young lady named Emma Golding who really knew her stuff and who understood Nathan's ultimate plan. She and her team worked diligently to get the fairest price possible and were largely successful in doing so.

Of course it takes quite a while to sell two hundred and fifty properties. In fact they spent the next three years doing just that. Initially, the selloff was covered by various news organizations that declared the death toll of the chain was underway. This suited Nathan just fine as he didn't want the public associating the new chain with the old one. But as they sold one and then another the company accumulated a lot of cash which would be used later to establish the new chain. Nathan and his team spent much of that time coming up with a new theme and design for the next generation of restaurants. They determined how much space would be needed, the exterior design to mark their restaurants, the ambience they wanted to achieve and the interior design to best accomplish that.

They then hired a core of head chefs to design the menu for the new chain. Focus groups were recruited to test their ideas and determine the best choices for the menu. This too was a multi-year project but eventually they had the new menu defined from appetizers to drinks, entrees and desserts.

In the third year they began buying new properties and building new restaurants according to their plan. The started with five locations in the most promising areas and launched the new enterprise. Grand openings were held in each after extensive advertising and the results were even better than expected. Nathan couldn't help but think back that all of his troubles had begun just as he opened the last restaurant of the old chain. But his focus was now on this latest endeavor and each location had success and turned a profit in their first year. Learning from these openings, additional locations were built. It wasn't easy but they were successful beyond even their own projections.

This process continued into a fourth year and then a fifth. Milestones were reached as they opened the first fifty restaurants and then the first one hundred. It was slow and steady but each year brought more success than the previous one and ten years later, Nathan attended the grand opening of his five hundredth location, twice the number he had under the old banner.

Success was of course wonderful, but best of all was the knowledge that God was the real key to his success. Nathan often paused and marveled at what all God had done and this new Nathan was known for his humility before God. Gone was the self-righteous captain of industry and in his place was a humble servant acknowledging God's grace at every step in his path to success. There were still occasional failures and challenges, but Nathan saw them as opportunities to grow and tried to convey that to his staff whenever possible. He never questioned God's motives for these tests when they came his way.

It was not only the business going through a major overhaul, but Nathan's personal life saw significant changes also. While Nathan was amazed at how God blessed the rebuilding of his business and financial success, he was in even more awe of how The Lord was blessing his home life.

# Chapter Nine

Any man would have taken note of Emma Golding, the lead real estate consultant retained by the company, and Nathan was no exception. She was indeed beautiful standing about 5'7" tall, with long brown hair that had a natural curl to her shoulders, dark brown eyes, a cute upturned nose and full lips. She was athletic in appearance and worked out regularly plus taking Zumba classes three mornings a week. Her long legs, thin waist and ample breasts never failed to make men turn their heads as she walked by.

But Nathan soon learned that there was much more to Emma than just physical appearance. She was extremely intelligent. Her knowledge of real estate was impressive and made it easy to see why she was the lead consultant on her team. However she was not limited to real estate. She had an impressive knowledge of current events, history, culture and the latest developments in politics, science and social media. She could even quote the latest statistics on the local baseball, basketball and football clubs. He soon concluded that she was one of the most informed and engaging people he had ever known.

Several of the eligible bachelors in the company asked her out during her first year on the job and she went out with a select few of them, but never for more than one or two dates. Nathan however was still grieving the loss of his wife and family and though intrigued no end by her, he didn't really consider asking her out. By the end of that first year and into the second, friends started suggesting that he needed more of a social life. Life couldn't just be business all of the time. Finally he agreed to go to dinner with his old friend Eli Fox and his wife and he worked up his nerve to ask Emma to accompany him.

"This is just a social event and I would really like it if you accompanied me" he said. He then explained the situation and she responded that she would be pleased to come with him. "I don't want you to think this is a work-related obligation or anything" he said as he nervously fidgeted in his chair. It had been years since he had asked anyone on a date and even then he had always been awkward about it. "No, I understand Nathan and I think it sounds like a nice, fun evening."

It did turn out to be a fun evening. He and Eli laughed and told stories about their adventures as youth in high school and on baseball trips. Eli's wife and Emma hit it off and were immersed in their own conversation much of the time. Toward the end of their meal a live band took the stage and Eli and his wife got up to dance along with half a dozen other couples. "Well, I'm not much of a dancer and I bet you are" said Nathan. "But if you'd like to chance it, I'll show you my best ballroom style." Soon they were up and dancing alongside Eli and his spouse. It was hard to tell whether Eli or Nathan was the worse dancer, but by the third song no one cared. They danced for thirty minutes or so and then returned to their table, winded and sweaty but with big smiles all around.

After that night Nathan asked Emma out a second time with just the two of them going to dinner. It wasn't until the third date that he dared to kiss her goodnight as he walked her to her door. It was a simple and quick kiss, but it had electricity to it that they both felt. As their relationship deepened he learned more about Emma and was delighted to learn that she was a devout believer. He had continued to attend the same church as before his disasters, and he appreciated the support the members had given him. She attended with him one Sunday and he attended her church the next Sunday. He found her church service refreshing with more modern music, a very relevant message, and generally speaking a younger congregation than his. The following week they returned to her church again and he found himself debating if it was time for a change. One evening the week after that he visited his pastor and told him that he was going to change membership. He wanted to assure the pastor that nothing was wrong and he had very much enjoyed his years there, but that he felt moved to try a new venue. The pastor assured him that he only wanted Nathan to follow the Spirit's leadership and there were no hard feelings. They prayed and he wished Nathan well at the new church. The decision made, Nathan soon started taking part in a weekly bible study in the new facility and felt he had made the right decision.

It was roughly a year and half after that first dinner date that Nathan and Emma married and started a new chapter in their lives. It was another fourteen months when their first child was born, a son name Joshua. He was followed a year later by Matthew, and two years after that Martha arrived on the scene. Nathan was again amazed at God's blessing after the birth of each child. He knew from his first family how precious children were and dedicated himself to being the best father he could be. From teaching Josh and Matthew how to catch and throw a baseball to taking a four-year old Martha to her first ballet class, he proved to be one of the best dads around. He was still committed to his business and its success but family always came first.

By the time Martha was ten years old he had the largest and most successful restaurant chain in America and every venture he entered into seemed to be blessed by God. He often stopped and thought back on his life and how God's hand had played a part in each season of his life. He still grieved for his first family and took comfort in knowing they were enjoying eternity, but he also took untold pleasure in his current circumstances and knew only God's grace enabled it.

As the years passed he turned more and more of his business over to his faithful management team. He also engaged Josh and Matthew in the business, letting them start as busboys and working their way up so that the time eventually came when they also began to take over some of his duties and become leaders in their own right. Martha also achieved success but took a different path. She went to law school and became an attorney who worked as a public defender. His children in turn repaid him and Emma with seven grandchildren and then years later with five great-grandchildren. These little rug rats became the golden crown of their older years.

# Chapter Ten

When Nathan was younger he had never thought that he would ever be a grandfather, much less a great grandfather. But as his years advanced and his business duties declined, he discovered that despite all of his other success the role of grandpa was the one he loved the most. He and Emma were careful to not get overly involved. They had to let the younger people be the parents, and yet still stay actively engaged in their grandchildren's lives. Sometimes this was a thin line but they strived to never cross it as the grands grew up. But there were certain things that Nathan made a point to share with each of the children when they reached an age of understanding.

At this time he would arrange to take the child out to dinner or to the zoo or some other activity where they could be alone and have an opportunity for a talk just between the two of them. These talks would go something like this. "Life is not a bed of roses kiddo, it's not fair. No matter who or what you become, you will have problems in life, difficulties that you can't explain, and hurts that will make you better or bitter. When these things happen, you will either grow up or give up. You may very well even become angry with God during those times. In the end you'll either become who God wants you to be or your heart will become hard. You have to decide how you are going to respond to the tough times in your life. How will you handle it? I encourage you when those times come to remember that he is God, he loves you and he cares for you. Hard as it may be, welcome these problems as trials, like hard workouts at the gym or the subject in school that you hate the most. These things test you but in the end make you stronger. And whatever else you do when you overcome these trials, don't get all pompous and proud of yourself. Remember it was God who got you through it and not yourself."

They did indeed experience hardships and trials. These came in many forms from personal relationships to school problems to business issues to moral dilemmas. One of his grandsons even spent time in prison for defrauding investors in a business venture. But Nathan was pleased and thankful that he and the others came through their trials stronger than before. He couldn't help but think that maybe those talks had made a difference in the kids' lives.

Nathan lived to a ripe old age before passing on to the next life. He was thankful for the love of Emma and his family. He was thankful to see all of his children and grandchildren become believers and lead devout lives. To his last breath he was in awe of the grace God had shown him. Emma lived for another ten years before joining Nathan. The children could only imagine the party they must have had in heaven.

# Epilogue

This story is based on the Old Testament book of Job. Job is not an easy book to read. A lot of people probably read the first two chapters to see the unbelievable tragedies that beset Job when God allowed Satan to test him, and then skip to the last chapter to find the relatively happy ending. In between Job and his friends engage in long conversations about the nature of God and how he deals with those who believe in and honor Him and those who do not. These conversations become quite contentious at times and address characteristics of God that people still debate today.

The biblical account opens by describing Job as a wealthy man with a wonderful family. It then switches to a scene where Satan visits God in heaven after roaming around the earth. God asks Satan if he has considered his servant Job and Satan essentially challenges Job's loyalty to God and says if he suffered losses of wealth and family that he would turn against God. God allows him to test this theory. In our story this conversation is portrayed by the television reporter Lucas Ferrano (Satan) and the cameraman (God). Nathan Jobe (Job) loses everything he has; he loses his home, his family and his business. As if that were not enough, he then personally suffers as sores break out all over his body. Despite this unbelievable pain and suffering he still acknowledges God.

In the Bible Job is soon visited by his friends Eliphaz (Eli Fox), Bildad (Billy DaPointe) and Zophar (Zack Parr). They are joined by a younger man named Elihu (Elon Hunt). Despite their good intentions these men all conclude that Job must have committed terrible sins to deserve this severe punishment from

God. Of course none of them are aware of the heavenly conversation between God and Satan. Job listens to them and consistently responds that he has committed no sin grievous enough to warrant such punishment. As the conversation continues they discuss views on the nature of God and how he deals with the just and the unjust.

We often hear the expression "the patience of Job" but he actually lost his patience with his friends several times as they continued to accuse him. Job, and Nathan, insisted that if he could just speak with God directly and present his case that he could justify himself. While Job may not have always been patient, he did exhibit admirable endurance and perseverance that sets a great example for all of us. Even with all the loss, all the pain and the accusations of his friends he never turned against God as Satan had claimed he would.

Job, and Nathan, very likely held views very similar to his friends at the beginning of the book. But as the story progresses we see a gradual transformation of his understanding. After wrestling with both his friends and with God, he realizes that while he may not have committed a specific sin that caused all his troubles, he was guilty of pride and had become quite self-righteous. As the story concludes he acknowledges that God is supreme and while we don't always know the reasons for what happens in our lives, we can rest in the assurance that He is in control and He loves us. Finally we, just as Nathan, can accept these events as opportunities, or tests that enable us to grow and deepen our faith. Is this easy? No, but with God's help we can do it.

# Rooted

by
*Bobby J Watson*

*What is firmly rooted*
*cannot be pulled out*

**Lao Tzu**


*Therefore as you have received*
*Christ Jesus the Lord, so walk in*
*Him, having been firmly rooted*
*and now being built up in Him*
*and established in your faith.....*

**Colossians 2:6-7**

**NASB 1995**

# Chapter One

"Yes Mom, I getting ready now and I will be there" Ethan almost shouted into the phone he held in one hand while he tried to button his shirt with the other hand. "Now, why are we doing this again?" He knew the answer but he wanted his Mom to restate it. He turned on the speaker and laid the phone down as he now put on his dress shoes. He and his wife Sabrina listened as his mother explained that she and all of her children were attending church today with their Grandma, her mother. Grandma Ruth was celebrating her 85th birthday and had asked that everyone go to church with her instead of buying gifts. She had assured them that would be the best gift of all. Ethan said "Mom, you know we don't go to church" as he finished tying his shoes. "I know you don't but this is for Grandma. You know how much she has done for all of us." He couldn't deny that as she had always been there for her grandchildren, picking them up from school, taking them to piano lessons or baseball or soccer practice. Whatever the activity she had never let them down as she helped raise them while their mother Elizabeth, a single mom, had worked. She had even baby sat their son Matthew and daughter Melanie on occasion. "Okay, just the one time and just for her but don't expect me to make a habit of it" he said as he hung up the phone.

Across town Violet, Ethan's younger sister, dragged herself out of bed after the alarm sounded for the third time. She knew she couldn't hit the snooze button again if she was going to be on time. She didn't really mind going to church, especially for Grandma Ruth, but why did they have to hold services so early? Who does anything at 10:30 on Sunday morning? Just then she got a text from Ethan asking if she was up and she sent him back a thumb up emoji. He replied that if he had to go to church, she did too. He wasn't going to be alone.

# ROOTED

It had been a late night partying with friends but as she got in the shower and the hot water started pounding her body she began to awaken and feel alive again. As she shampooed and lathered herself she thought about Grandma Ruth. She was the only girl in the family of three brothers and her mother was always working while they were growing up it seemed. So Grandma Ruth had been the one to help her with homework, to take her to cheerleader practice, to be her confidant when her first boyfriend gave her a nervous kiss. She loved Grandma Ruth and would do anything for her, but she had long ago left church behind. She smiled to herself as she realized that Grandma Ruth was the only person for whom she would make this early morning sacrifice. Shower finished, she put on her most modest dress and began to apply her makeup. Looking at the time she realized she needed to leave in the next ten minutes.

Robert lived in an upscale suburban neighborhood where the HOA insisted on three trees being in every front yard, enforced a ban on cars parked overnight on the streets and was quick to send a letter if you failed to keep your yard mowed. He and his wife April owned a two story, five bedroom home on a corner lot that was easily one of the largest in the neighborhood. He used one bedroom as an office where he often spent long nights fulfilling his duties as Assistant to the Chief Financial Officer of a large accounting firm. Two of the other bedrooms belonged to their two sons, Anthony and Edward who were eight and six respectively. He now finished tying his necktie and then stepped into April's dressing room to see if she was ready to go. The boys were already dressed and watching cartoons on TV in the family room. He was anxious that they get to the church service on time. It wasn't so much about excitement for the service as it was his competitive nature. Ever since he was a kid he had striven to outdo his brother Ethan at whatever they were doing. It didn't matter if it was grades at school, being the best hitter on the baseball team, or being the first to arrive at church, he was determined to beat Ethan. So today they got in their Mercedes SUV and drove toward the church and he felt like he would surely be the first one there. Of course he reminded himself that the ultimate goal today was to please Grandma Ruth, but beating Ethan came in a very close second.

Jason lived in a much different neighborhood than his older brother Robert. He and his wife Emily lived a few miles outside of town in a rural area. They had a 3-bedroom ranch style house on a two-acre plot of land. Most of their neighbors owned similar lots that ranged from an acre or two up to ten acres. A few had cows, horses and chickens but many like Jason just enjoyed having the open space. The neighbors were all friendly, never failing to wave when they encountered each other on the road and occasionally one would host a party and grill burgers for everyone. There were still a few large farms in the area where corn or cotton was grown and in the last year a housing development had started constructing new homes. None of the current residents were enthusiastic about this, but they clung to the hope that the area would remain essentially as it was.

Jason loved Grandma Ruth very much and while he and Emily didn't really attend church, he was happy to do whatever to please Grandma on this special birthday. He and Emily had married two years earlier and they had plans for kids in the future. He had mused that when that happened perhaps they would find a church in the area. After all it was good for kids to have some guidance and structure and church could help with that. But for now they enjoyed their downtime on Sundays. After all he commuted twenty miles into town for his job every weekday and it was nice to just do nothing on the weekends.

He finished dressing and walked into the living/den where Emily was watching one of the morning shows on television. She looked beautiful in the new dress she had bought for the occasion. She arose and turned off the TV when he entered the room. He gave her a kiss and they climbed into their Ford F150 pickup and started the 30-minute trek to church. As he drove he thought about Grandma Ruth. Being the youngest in the family he had always been a little spoiled and knew it. He smiled as he remembered how Grandma had done more than her share of that spoiling. It would be good to see her again, and what the heck maybe the church service would even be interesting. Who knows?

# Chapter Two

Robert pulled into the church parking lot and was pleased not to see Ethan's BMW anywhere. As a matter of fact he didn't see his Mom's car either which meant they must literally be the first of the group to arrive. He couldn't restrain a smug smile as he considered that he had beaten everyone. Finding a parking spot, he turned around toward the backseat where his boys were both playing games on their tablets. He said to them and April, "Well looks like we're the first to arrive. We'll wait in the car until someone else shows up." It didn't take long. Two or three minutes later his mother pulled up and parked beside him. They were all getting out and exchanging hugs when Ethan zoomed in and parked in an isolated spot near them, obviously hoping nobody would park near his car. He hated getting door dings on his new BMW M3 sedan.

Their mother, Elizabeth, looked very pretty in her new dress and they all told her so. But Grandma Ruth was absolutely radiant. She was visibly overjoyed that they had all shown up and couldn't contain her happiness. After greeting each other they stood in the lot and talked for a few minutes and then Jason and Emily arrived. Jason parked and practically ran over to his grandma and gave her a hug and kiss on the cheek. He then hugged his mom and April, Sabrina and all the kids before shaking hands with Robert and Ethan. It had been a while since they had all seen one another and it really was good to see everyone. They started walking toward the church building and were about to enter when someone shouted "Hey! Wait for me!" They all turned and saw Violet running in her high heels toward them. Another round of hugs and hellos and then they walked into the church foyer.

Suddenly it was like they were the entourage for a rock star. Everyone they met hugged and greeted Elizabeth and especially Grandma Ruth. She would speak to them, often asking about their family members or maybe a prayer request they had mentioned and then she would introduce her family to them. She absolutely beamed with pride as she did so. Everyone shook their hands and greeted them cordially. Another round of hugs and "Happy Birthdays" ensued when Elizabeth informed the congregants why the family was attending that day. The love that everyone had for Grandma Ruth was so obvious.

They slowly made their way through the foyer and into the auditorium where they found an unoccupied row and took their seats. The service started soon afterward, beginning with music by the choir which served as a call to worship ushering everyone in to take their seats. But before everyone was even seated the choir director had them stand and he led the congregation in two hymns, How Great Thou Art and When We All Get to Heaven. Then they were seated again and the Praise Team, backed by the choir, did a final number before the Pastor prayed for the service. After his prayer ended, he led the congregation in The Lord's Prayer.

The stage now set, the Pastor went to the lectern and began his sermon. Sermons come in a number of varieties. Many times they are intended more for regular members than for newcomers or unbelievers and they carry a message to help build up or edify the members, to help them become more mature in their Christian journey. Sometimes they address sensitive issues within the church body if there is some type of dissension. And of course there are those sermons that remind the members to be cheerful givers and increase the church's revenue. After all every church has bills to pay, ministries to finance and staff on payroll. Today's sermon however was none of those. It was an evangelistic homily that was addressed mostly to non-believers, although it was always good for believers to hear again too.

The Pastor started by documenting man's situation before a holy God. There were of course many degrees of sin but just one sin was enough to separate us from the Heavenly Father. He quoted from Isaiah 53:6 and Romans 3:23 which both tell us that we are all sinners. All have gone astray and gone our own way as Psalm 53:3 makes very clear. There is not a one of us who is righteous on his own merits. Yes, man was in quite a pickle.

But then God provided a way of deliverance, a road to salvation for us. The Pastor then explained how hundreds of years before Christ, Isaiah 7:14 promised and foretold that a virgin would give birth and his name would be Immanuel or "God with us". John 3:16 tells us that Jesus was that child, God's own son, and all who believe in him will not only have their sins forgiven but will inherit eternal life. To conclude he pointed out that Jesus said in John 14:6 that he was the way, the truth, and the life and that only through him could someone come to know the Father. He was the way.

It was a powerful sermon. Even a non-believer who chose to ignore the message had to admire the presentation skills of the Pastor. He was an excellent speaker who knew just when to raise his voice and when to lower it to a whisper. He moved about the stage in a way that compelled all eyes to follow him. He displayed an uncanny ability to look everyone in the eye at the same time. Any public speaker would have praised his ability and his technique.

As the service ended he made a final plea for everyone to consider their personal situation before God, to assure themselves that they had placed their trust in Jesus. He made it clear that anyone not affiliated with a local church would find a welcome home at this one. This church did not have an invitation where people were asked to come forward and make their decisions public. Instead the Pastor encouraged anyone who had made a decision or who had questions to indicate it on a connection card and turn it in as part of the offering. He or another minister would contact them privately about their decision and any next steps to take. He then made a final prayer and ended it with "Lord, I've sown the seed to the best of my ability. Please bless the harvest." The ushers passed the offering plates down each row and the choir led everyone in a final hymn.

Making their way out of the building was not as difficult as their entrance had been, but there were still several people who stopped them to shake hands and invite them to come again. After their exit everyone drove to Grandma's favorite restaurant where they enjoyed a meal together and Elizabeth surprised Grandma by presenting a cake with two large numbers, 8 and 5, atop it. It was carrot cake which was her favorite and everyone raved about it as they enjoyed a piece. Then they said their good-byes and each made their way back home.

Grandma Ruth had tears of joy in her eyes as everyone kissed her and said good-bye. It had been a good day and a great birthday.

# Chapter Three

Ethan sat down after they sang the last of the two opening hymns and looked at his watch. He had plans for the afternoon and hoped the preacher wouldn't drag things out too long. He listened to the first few words of the sermon and thought to himself *I've heard this stuff before. We're all sinners, all terrible people, blah blah blah.* He looked around the congregation and studied the faces of people sitting in the pews. *It's amazing what people will believe,* he thought to himself. He didn't for a minute buy into these myths and legends about some god who created everything and knew everything and existed everywhere and judged everything. And even if that were all true, how could someone else die for the sins of everybody else? But as he looked around, he could see that the poor souls in the auditorium were eating it up. He guessed it gave them some sense of relief from mistakes they had made or something like that.

He then looked down his own pew and saw that everyone in his family seemed to be entranced by this message too. He could understand Grandma Ruth believing. After all she had been raised her whole life to believe it and she had limited education. His mother Elizabeth had also been raised in it her whole life. But Robert and April seemed to be hanging on to every word too and Robert should certainly know better. Maybe he was just putting on appearances for Grandma's sake. Jason was also very attentive and he noticed that he was even writing notes on the program they had been given when they entered the auditorium. Well, Jason had always been the youngest and the favorite so he would want Grandma Ruth to think he was really taking this in. Even Violet sat rapt in attention listening to this message and Ethan was pretty sure she had been out partying the night before until the wee hours of the morning. It was a wonder she was even able and sober enough to get up and be here. Oh well, they could put on all the show they wanted. He would sit and be polite until this thing was over and then he had better things to do.

As he did so he remembered how even when he was child and Grandma Ruth had taken them to Vacation Bible School he really wasn't that interested except that he did like to play the games and take part in any sports contest they had. This religion stuff had never been for him.

Just then Sabrina nudged him and nodded toward their children who were both playing games on their cell phones. Although he assumed that Sabrina wanted him to tell them to put down the devices, he actually found it humorous. They at least were as uninterested as he was and after all they weren't hurting anyone. So instead he whispered to them to "be sure your phones are on mute". Matthew was the oldest grandchild at thirteen and gave his dad a scowl that said "Duh, do you think I'm an idiot?" He had entered those terrible teenage years and didn't respond well to any type of authority. His grades had also begun to suffer as he tended to ignore homework and failed to study for tests. Jason figured this was just a phase and he would emerge from it after a while. Melanie on the other hand was daddy's little girl and immediately smiled and showed that her phone was on mute. She was eleven and had pretty much had Jason wrapped around her finger since birth as only little girls can do to their dads.

The preacher seemed to be wrapping up his homily and was now pleading for everyone to come to Jesus. Ethan was glad this wasn't one of those churches that dragged out the invitation with piano playing in the background while the preacher begged and begged. He was also glad that it wasn't a church where people walked down the aisle when they had made a decision. This always led to personal speeches about their life and then an obligatory line of handshaking to congratulate them. So when the pastor asked everyone to bow for prayer he was actually glad to do it because it meant the service was truly close to ending. Of course first there must be the offering.

He again found himself looking around as the offering plates were passed. Nowadays a lot of parishioners paid their tithe online so the plates were mostly for the connection cards plus a few checks and cash. Still he couldn't help but think as the plate came down their aisle about the words of the old circus owner P.T. Barnum that a sucker was born every minute. And to him this was pretty much like a circus with its performers and promises of miracles and so forth. He smiled to himself as he plucked two dollar bills down on the plate and passed it on to his kids who in turn passed it down the aisle. He knew that he was just donating to a fairy tale, unlike these other chumps and he only did it for Grandma Ruth's sake. He looked to his left and was met with another scowl from Sabrina who seemed disappointed or maybe just embarrassed that he had offered such a small amount.

When they exited the auditorium he made an excuse and immediately rushed out of the building to his car where he waited on everyone else. He knew that everyone would again be stopping them to shake hands and wish Grandma Ruth a happy birthday and he was anxious to get out of that building instead of wading through it with everyone else. When the others came out they agreed on a place for lunch and got in their cars. Matthew and Melanie immediately put on headphones and continued with their games or music or whatever they had going on their phones.

Sabrina loudly slammed her door shut and said in obvious anger "You know, you could have at least acted like you were interested. You looked more like a spoiled brat who had been told to sit in the corner".

"You knew I didn't want to come. I only did it for Grandma. Besides everyone else was so into the message they probably didn't notice me anyway."

"I sure hope you're right. Grandma and Elizabeth are both wonderful people and they deserve better from their children."

"Well whatever, it's over now. Let's go have lunch, give Grandma her gift and then I have things to do."

"I'm sure you do" she responded as they followed the others to the restaurant.

On their way to the restaurant Melanie suddenly yanked off her earphones and said "Daddy, look at all those birds over there! What are they doing? There's like hundreds of them."

They were on a new stretch of road where the highway department had just completed a project to add a third lane to accommodate the heavy traffic this road typically saw during the week. The project had seemingly lasted forever and during the last phase they had planted grass seed along a high embankment next to the new lane.

"Well sugar, they just planted grass on that hill next to the road and some of the seed rolled down to the shoulder. It will never grow on that hard gravelly ground and the birds are eating it up."

"Wow that's so cool! I never saw so many birds in one place" she said excitedly.

Soon after that they pulled into the restaurant parking lot and went inside where a room had been reserved for their party.

## Chapter Four

They were ushered into a private room at the restaurant where Grandma and Elizabeth along with Robert and his family had already seated themselves. They took seats across the table from Robert, April and the kids. Jason and Emily arrived next and took seats next to the kids and opposite each other. Violet then came in and seated herself at the opposite end of the table from Grandma Ruth. The restaurant had a full menu so there was plenty of thoughtful perusing before making a choice. Finally Ethan ordered a cheeseburger and fries for Matthew, macaroni and cheese for Melanie, rib eye steak and a baked potato for Sabrina and prime rib with asparagus spears for himself. They all settled on soda to drink. He might normally have ordered a different drink but Grandma preferred no alcohol at the table. The others ordered as well and then the guest of honor stood and told everyone how much she loved each of them and how much she appreciated that they had come to church with her today. She hoped they would choose to attend again. She then raised her glass of water in a toast to everyone.

Various conversations ensued as they waited on their food. Ethan mostly watched and listened as the others told Grandma how much they had enjoyed the service. Finally she asked him what he had thought and he simply said "it was quite interesting. I thought the music was good." Thankfully food arrived not long afterward and he was spared from other comments on the topic. After enjoying the meal and birthday cake, he and the family drove home where he quickly changed clothes and told Sabrina that he had a golfing date with some buddies and would be back later that evening.

He breathed a sigh of relief as he drove to the golf course and met his fellow golfers. This was what Sunday afternoons were for, not sitting in stuffy churches and hearing about some kind of savior. He apologized to his friends for being a bit late and explained the reason. They nodded and laughed, recalling when they had been roped into similar situations. He then went on to shoot a 10 over par which was one of his better rounds ever and so he paid for the drinks at the 19th hole that day.

In the months ahead Ethan never thought again about that morning, but instead focused on his job and other activities. He and Sabrina seemed to drift apart during that time. They had once been almost inseparable, doing almost everything together. Now they were more like roommates than husband and wife. They didn't argue or have disagreements or anything like that. They just each went their own way and seldom talked except for necessities about the house or other matters. It reached a point where he moved to an unused bedroom upstairs, explaining to Matthew and Melanie that he snored so loud at night that their mom couldn't sleep.

Melanie said "Gosh Daddy, I hope you don't keep me awake. I'm just in the next room."

"Don't worry, sweetie. I'll make sure my door is shut" he replied with a smile.

Meanwhile Matthew's grades continued to decline. He spent most of his time on his phone or tablet playing video games or hanging out with his friends. Sabrina told Ethan that she was concerned about his friends and believed they were not a good influence. She begged Ethan to talk to Matthew, but he told her it was just a phase. Matthew was a good kid and would straighten himself out sooner or later. Truth was that he didn't really know what to say to his son and figured Sabrina could handle it better than him. He became a little more concerned when Matthew brought a girl home to dinner one night. He was now fourteen and she was his first real girlfriend. He had asked Sabrina if she could come to dinner and of course Sabrina said yes. As they ate that night Ethan marveled that his son was now old enough to be into girls. Even more amazing was the news that she attended a local church and Matthew had started attending their youth group. Ethan thought to himself *great now I have a Holy Roller right here in the house.* The good news however was that Matthew's grades started to improve again so Ethan concluded this was all okay as long as Matthew didn't start preaching to them at home.

Not that Ethan was home that much anyway. He spent more and more time at his job where he was a Project Manager for a software company. The job was going well even if his home life wasn't. He would typically put in nine or ten hours there and then go to a sports bar close by where several friends met almost every evening. Some sport was always in season and they had decent food in addition to beer or wine to drink. A normal night saw him stay there to 10:30 or so and then he would head home where everyone was already in bed and he would crash in his upstairs bedroom. Tomorrow was another day.

He and Sabrina never got a divorce. Maybe someday when Matthew and Melanie were out of college and on their own that would happen. But for now they just coexisted and led their own lives. They attended family events for birthdays, Christmas, school activities and the like together and put on their best appearance. Two or three times a year they would meet with the extended family and share a meal or an afternoon together. They even went on a couple of family vacations, one road trip and one cruise. But in each of these scenarios they were simply doing their duty. It had evolved into a loveless marriage and was destined to stay that way.

Sometimes after everyone else had left work and headed home, Ethan would sit in his top-floor office and stare out the window. At those times he would often wonder what it was all about. What was life all about after all? There really seemed to be no real purpose to it. You lived, you did the best you could, you raised your kids, sometimes you had some fun, but it just didn't seem to have much purpose otherwise. He wondered if other people felt the same way. It was like there must be more, but he didn't know what it was.

Then he would make his way to the sports bar for food, drink and companionship. Tomorrow was another day.

## Chapter Five

Violet pulled into the church parking lot in a near panic. She didn't want to be late and yet she had left her apartment later than intended. She had gone to the party of a friend last night with good intentions. She would stay and have a good time, but she would make her excuse and leave no later than 11:30 PM. That would give her time to drive home and be in bed by midnight. That had been the plan, but the booze was flowing and the music was so loud and great. She loved to dance and some fellow named Brian proved the perfect partner. He had great moves and was such a gentleman, always ensuring her glass was never empty as they rested between dances. So she saw 11:30 come and go and then midnight. Finally a little after 2:00 AM a few people started leaving and she forced herself to do the same. She promised Brian that he had not seen the last of her. So it was 2:30 or a little later when she crashed in her bed and the alarm going off at 9:00 AM was not a welcome sound. Hitting snooze three times she finally dragged herself to the shower about 9:30. Rushing like she seldom did she had made it to the church just a few minutes before 10:30. She really didn't want to make a scene coming in late and felt a rush of relief upon seeing Grandma Ruth and the others heading toward the door as she pulled into the parking lot.

A flood of memories came to her as she and the others walked through the building toward their seats. This was the church where Grandma had taken them to Vacation Bible School. She remembered how much fun she had coloring pictures and playing with the other children. And she recalled how much she had loved hearing the bible stories. For some reason she especially remembered the story of the little man Zaccheus who had climbed a sycamore tree to see Jesus as he walked along in a great crowd. She remembered that Jesus not only saw him but had dinner at his house. She didn't remember why but everyone hated

Zaccheus, everyone that was except Jesus who was so kind to him. She wondered why that story resonated so much with her as they took their seats in the auditorium.

The church auditorium was just as she remembered it, although it had seemed much larger to her as a child. Violet loved to sing and she had a pretty nice voice. She sang along in her best alto to How Great Thou Art and then she really got into singing When We All Get to Heaven. She looked at the others as she was singing and saw that Grandma Ruth and her Mom were both singing loudly and didn't even look at the words. They knew these songs so well. Robert and April were also singing pretty loudly and seemingly enjoying themselves. Jason and Emily were doing about the same, as was Sabrina. Ethan however was just mouthing the words. She doubted she would have heard him if she had been standing right next to him. She knew that he didn't want to be here and it showed as she looked at his face.

They sat down for the sermon and she braced herself to hear it. She knew that she was far from perfect and the Pastor might very well step on her toes with his words, but she was here for Grandma Ruth and she would endure whatever he said. She listened dutifully at first but then more attentively as he got into his delivery. She was intrigued by his saying that none of them, no one in that large room, was perfect and that it didn't matter how many sins you had committed. Whether you had one sin or a million, you were not perfect enough for God on your own merits. She might be a party animal but she was no dummy. She knew that she had plenty that needed forgiving and his explanation struck a nerve with her and the thought that everyone was in the same situation was almost a relief. He then explained how Jesus was God's own son and had come to earth with just one purpose and that was to pay for her sin and the sin of everyone who believed. That seemed too simple but the pastor pointed to scripture that said that acceptance of Jesus was in fact the only way to be forgiven.

Violet became lost in her thoughts, in a sense of reverie, as the sermon continued. Yes, she knew she was far, far from perfect. She had started out on a pretty good track but in high school she fell in with a crowd that loved to drink and party. She started missing curfew and staying out later and later, eventually staying out all night at times. She loved the adrenalin rush, the excitement that dancing and laughing gave her. And the alcohol helped bring that on quicker and more deeply. Then one of her girlfriends offered her some pills one night and told her they made things even more fun. So she popped a couple and woke up the next morning at that friend's house, not sure what had transpired after taking the pills.

She managed to finish high school with the sympathetic help of a couple of teachers and started college. College offered even more freedom and her partying became almost nonstop until she flunked out during her second semester. Since then she had found jobs mostly in retail sales. Currently she was a salesperson at a high end dress shop. Her life had not really changed however except now she usually limited the partying to weekends in order to keep from losing her job. She didn't consider herself an addict or alcoholic but she loved to drink and didn't turn down the occasional snort of coke or a little meth if it was offered to her. She had of course found herself waking up in the bed of many different men during those times and there was one consequence that no one in her family had ever known. A couple of years earlier she had missed her period and found out she was pregnant. She had the pregnancy terminated as quickly as possible and had never told a soul about it. During her more somber moments she often wondered what that child would have been like. Would it have had her hair, her eyes? Would it have had the sweet disposition of Grandma Ruth? She wondered.

But now as she listened to the Pastor she heard the message that she could be free from the pain and guilt that plagued her in quieter moments. Her heart almost leaped for joy when he said that in Christ we could all be new creatures, new people. For the first time in so long she saw the possibility and dreamed of a different life that was governed by more than momentary pleasure. She sprang happily from her seat to sing that final hymn.

Yes! She could have a new life! Today was the beginning of something wonderful and special!

She hugged Grandma Ruth when they reached their cars and told her how much she had enjoyed this and thanked her for inviting all of them to church. She smiled, no she practically giggled all the way to the restaurant, recalling bits and pieces of the sermon and the wonderful hymns they had sung.

## Chapter Six

Violet returned to her apartment that day after lunch with the family. She took a three hour nap which really restored her energy. She was still riding a new kind of high, a spiritual high, and searched through her bookshelf and then the drawers of her dresser until she finally found a Bible that her mother had given her years before. She had taken notes during the sermon that morning and now she looked up those scriptures and read them again. Yes, they read just as the Pastor had said. She retained that sense of liberation that had struck her that morning. She just knew that this was indeed a new beginning for her. She read through the passages again and then found the story about Zaccheus and read it twice. She felt a little like Zaccheus. It had been difficult for her to see Jesus and maybe people looked down on her, but Jesus would gladly have dinner with her.

She happily reported to work Monday morning with a spring in her step. Her happiness showed and some of her coworkers noticed it. One, a young lady named Laura asked "So what's going on, Violet? You seem too happy for a Monday morning." She told her about the day before and how wonderful it had all been and how it had really uplifted her spirit.

"I really plan to make some changes, Laura."

"Oh, it's one of those church things, huh? Violet, please don't tell me you're going to turn into one of those bible thumpers. Things are boring enough around here already without you quoting scripture at us."

Violet didn't know just what a bible thumper was and she really didn't know how to respond. Obviously Laura didn't understand what had happened to her. She certainly didn't want to cause any trouble. Maybe later she would be able to explain it better to Laura. But for now she just said, "Oh no, nothing like that. No worries."

She finished out her day and picked up some fast food for dinner, returning to her apartment about 7:00 PM. Her apartment was on the third floor and had a small balcony with a nice view of the surrounding countryside. It had a chair and small table and she sat there to eat her dinner. It was a pleasant place to dine; it was peacefully quiet and she enjoyed watching the sunset. The sun today had a nice reddish orange tint as it hovered over the nearby hills. On one of the closer hillsides she noticed that a number of pink wild daisies had popped up overnight and were nestled in the rocky terrain. She smiled as she admired how they dotted the area and added a welcome dash of color to the hillside.

The next day at work she didn't mention her experience from Sunday and Laura didn't bring it up either. She just set about getting through the day, selling six evening gowns which was actually not a bad day's result for Tuesday. She continued through the rest of week in the same manner and her thoughts turned less and less to the previous weekend. Saturday turned out to be a very busy day and everyone stayed occupied from opening to closing time. It was almost always their busiest day but this Saturday was brutal by comparison to most. They barely had time to scarf down their lunches between customers and often were helping two or three customers at a time. Everyone was glad to see the doors close that evening.

Violet was picking up her purse and other belongings and planned to return home and crash when her cell phone rang. It was Meghan, one of her closest friends, and she was calling to remind her about a party at Meghan's place that night. It had been scheduled for some time but Violet had totally forgotten it. *What should I do,* she pondered. She still had the dream born last weekend of making changes in her life, but Meghan was such a good friend. She didn't want to disappoint her. She decided that *yes, I'll go but just for a while. I'll eat, speak to everyone, and then make an excuse to leave.*

She arrived at Meghan's about 9:00 PM just as things were getting underway. As expected there was a nice buffet (Meghan always had a nice buffet) with a broad selection of food and she filled a plate and took a seat on the sofa. She had poured herself a soda to drink with the meal. She was enjoying the meal and just the opportunity to sit and relax after her busy day when who should walk in the door to Meghan's apartment but Brian. He saw her right away and came over to sit by her. They exchanged greetings and he went and filled a plate and returned.

She kept trying to think of an excuse to leave soon but nothing was coming to mind. Then the music started. People began to pair up and dance. They had both now finished their plates and Brian stood and offered his hand, inviting her to dance. *Oh, dear. I shouldn't do this but he's such a good dancer and so good looking too. Maybe just one dance.* Several dances later they fell back onto the sofa to catch their breath, both unable to hold back their laughter. They were having such a good time. Brian went and got a beer and a glass of wine for her. He had remembered that she was particularly fond of Malbec. It did taste good and helped restore her energy for the next round of dances. Brian made sure she had a fresh glass each time they took a break. He was such a gentleman!

A few people started leaving around midnight but by then she and Brian were having far too good a time to leave. The music boomed and wine flowed. After that initial exodus Meghan's boyfriend produced a line of cocaine that Violet snorted along with Meghan, her boyfriend and a few others. Brian declined saying he would stay clear headed and drive her home later. He had drunk a few beers but had not indulged as much as most of them had. About 2:30 AM he did indeed drive her home. She had to admit she had really had a great time and loved being with him so she asked if he wanted to stay the night, an invitation he quickly accepted.

She was dreaming a strange but pleasant dream of bunnies hopping along a trail on just their back legs when something jostled her. "Violet, Violet" she heard over and over until she finally opened her eyes. "Violet, I have to go now." It was Brian sitting beside her on the bed, already dressed. "I have to go babe, but I'll call you later" he said. She finally awakened just enough to say "Oh, okay. Last night was great."

"Yeah, it was. I'll call you later."

She reached up and kissed him and then lay back on her pillow. She heard the door close and was quickly asleep again, sleeping another three hours and finally getting out of bed a little after 1:00 PM. Staggering into the kitchenette she opened the refrigerator, poured a glass of orange juice, found three aspirin in the cabinet and walked out to her balcony where she sat at the table.

Looking at her cell phone she saw that Grandma Ruth had called sometime around noon. She had been too asleep to even hear it. Looking out over the balcony to the nearby hillside she was surprised to see that the wild daisies which had been blooming just the day before were now gone. The rocky terrain and sun had been too much for them. They had never taken root enough to survive. *Looks like they had about as much staying power as my revival. I was just born to be a party girl, I guess.* She went back inside after a while and spent the afternoon relaxing. She watched some television that evening and waited for Brian to call. He never did.

# Chapter Seven

Robert marveled at how many people came and hugged Grandma Ruth as they walked toward the auditorium. He knew how much he and the rest of the family loved her, but he had no idea that she had so many friends. Most of them didn't even know it was her birthday until they were told so this was the way she was normally greeted, not just special attention because of the day. Of course they all greeted the family enthusiastically and welcomed them to the service.

He remembered the church of course. They took their seat and he recalled coming here as a child. Grandma Ruth always made sure they attended Vacation Bible School when they were growing up and also Sunday School when their mom worked that day, but then as they entered their teen years they were more on their own while their Mom worked. Their attendance had pretty much stopped at that point. However he did recall returning to the sanctuary for weddings and a couple of funerals. Currently they did not attend anywhere and his own children had not experienced Sunday School or VBS. As a family they were pretty involved in sports and school functions and it was difficult to find time for everything. Still, he wondered if more exposure to religion might benefit his kids.

His wife April was a stay at home mom and was very much involved with their children's school. Anthony was in the third grade, while Edward was in the first and April was the President of the school's PTA chapter. Both she and Robert were also members of the local Country Club where Robert served on the board and April was on the Planning Committee that organized most of the Club's activities. Anthony played Little League Football in the fall and winter and baseball in the spring and summer. He had already told his dad that he wanted to start playing in the baseball Select League, often called Travel League, when he turned nine and became eligible to play in that league. Edward was not so much into those sports but he was the most aggressive soccer player on his team which consisted of 5 and 6 year olds.

Robert was earnestly devoted to his job and had plans to become Chief Financial Officer when his boss retired next year. He was equally devoted to his status in the community. This placed great importance on his role at the Country Club and his involvement in its activities which included a number of charitable events each year. But the primary reason for all of this devotion was his family. He dearly loved his family and wanted only the best for them. He wanted his boys to have every opportunity and was dedicated to seeing them succeed in life. Of course his love for April was second to none and he was just as determined to see her succeed in her endeavors.

So, all in all, it was a busy life but now as he stood and sung the first two hymns the thought occurred to him that perhaps he had neglected the spiritual aspect of life. He had taught his sons about right and wrong but could the teachings of the church supplement that? He remembered the moral lessons taught in Sunday School and he concluded that such teaching would be good for his boys. They were good lessons to learn. He then wondered how attending church regularly might benefit him and April. Being known as regular worshippers would certainly be an asset to them as they fulfilled their roles at school and the Country Club. It would probably even help some at work where the company president was a well-known church attender.

All of these thoughts flooded his mind as he sat down after singing the hymns. The preacher started his sermon and Robert found himself listening more and more intently. He noticed that April also seemed heavily invested in the pastor's words and he wondered what was going through her mind. If two people were ever equally minded it was him and April. They shared the same visions, the same hopes and dreams. They often found themselves laughing during conversations when they discovered that they both had the same thoughts, the same opinions and ideas. They even talked over each other, saying the exact same words. It was almost like they were one mind in two bodies. Disagreements sometimes happened but they were indeed very rare and usually short-lived.

Now as he listened to the sermon he realized there were even more reasons to consider coming to church more often. The pastor was exactly right when he said that all of us had made mistakes, had sinned. Robert was no fool. He knew that sometimes, despite his best intentions and efforts, he messed up and did things that were not right. Oh, he hadn't murdered anyone or robbed a bank, but he had definitely wished bad things on people and he knew this was wrong. And yes, he was not above a little cheating on his taxes and even a little cheating on the books at work to help the company look better. He had looked at other women and wished he could have a one-night stand with them. Okay, he actually had done that twice when he had been out of town at business conferences and had an extra drink or two while regaling with coworkers. So, he knew that indeed he was not perfect and certainly not innocent.

He also recalled from his childhood teachings that he could do nothing on his own to remove these sins. The words of the pastor now reminded him of this and the pastor also explained that the only way to have sins forgiven was through Jesus. He had taken our place and been punished for us on the cross. Tears welled in Robert's eyes now as he pondered this. While the choir sung its final hymn he determined that there needed to be some changes in his life and the life of his family. They needed to set some different priorities.

They all walked out together. When entering the service they had been greeted by members of the children's department who had taken the boys to Sunday School. April walked over and picked them up from their classrooms. Both boys had enjoyed their class and both had colored pictures based on bible studies they had heard in class. Anthony had learned about Jonah and the whale and had colored a picture showing the whale approaching the boat in which Jonah was a passenger. Edward had heard about David and Goliath and had a picture showing them confronting each other and David preparing to sling the rock at the giant. They were both excited and told April and then their dad about what they had learned.

Pulling out of the parking lot Robert said, "You know I think we should do this more often. What do you think?"

April replied, "I was thinking exactly the same thing" and they both started laughing. Here they were, thinking alike again.

They boys then piped in saying "Yay, it was fun. We want to come back!"

# Chapter Eight

Robert had a busy week after that day of worship and celebration. His company was going through an audit that was required for their annual stockholder's report. As Assistant to the Chief Financial Officer most of the legwork for this report fell to him. He was constantly in and out of the temporary office set up for the auditors, answering their questions and as was often the case meeting with various other employees to answer those questions. The audit normally took a couple of weeks and it always proved to be a hectic half-month. When it was all over the CFO would review the resulting report and sign off on it. Robert dreamed of the day when he could sit back and let someone else do the work while he simply read their conclusion and signed a document.

April was equally occupied with various duties that week. The kids' school was holding its annual fundraiser which amounted to giving each student an opportunity to win prizes by selling the most cookies. She prepared the explanatory letter that was sent to parents explaining how the contest worked and she also visited each classroom and pumped up the students' enthusiasm by describing the marvelous prizes they could win. Then after school she split her time between taking Anthony to baseball practice and Edward to soccer games. She would have sworn if asked that she had indeed met herself both coming and going.

The following Saturday rolled around and Robert informed her that he still had work to do on the audit and would be tied up all day. That left it to April to drive Anthony to his baseball game. The team was involved in a tournament and games were played on three different fields around town. After they won the first game she piled him and four other boys into her SUV and took them to a second field that was twenty minutes away for their next game. While that game was being played she picked up Edward from yet another soccer game. They had lost so she consoled him on the drive back to the baseball field.

Everyone returned home about the same time that evening. April pulled into the driveway at straight up 7:00 PM and Robert showed up about twenty minutes later. Beat and exhausted they opted for pizza delivery for dinner. The boys showered and were ready for bed by 9:00 PM. Robert and April crashed on the sofa in the den and mindlessly watched a real crime show on television. Retiring to their bedroom Robert said, "Well I hate to tell you this but I'll be working again all day tomorrow. These auditors this year are about to drive me nuts with their demands."

"That's too bad. Anthony's game is a 10:00 in the morning and I know he was hoping you could come. If they win, the championship game is a 1:00 in the afternoon."

"I'll talk with him in the morning. I think he'll understand. There's nothing I can do about it though. The work has to be done."

April then had that look like a light bulb had just come on. She said "guess that means church will have to wait until the following Sunday, huh?"

"Yes, I guess it will."

The next week was largely a repeat of that one. The auditors finally left on Thursday after the CFO reviewed and signed their final report. He then informed Robert and the rest of his staff that they, with Robert's leadership, would be responsible for putting together the annual report for the company. They had one month to produce the document before the stockholders' meeting and should expect to put in some overtime, including weekends, to get the job done on time.

Meanwhile April started receiving back the order forms from the students and was responsible to order the right number and flavor of cookies so the kids could deliver them to their customers as soon as possible. As if this didn't keep her busy enough she was also on the Planning Committee for the Country Club and was heavily involved in preparations for the annual Debutante Ball. This was a yearly event for the teenage children of the members. It was a formal affair with the boys wearing tuxedos and the girls modelling their trendiest ballroom gowns. Secretly she reckoned that the kids would have preferred wearing jeans and shorts and getting down to their own favorite bands. But this was really more for the parents who loved seeing their youngsters dress up and grace the dance floor to orchestra music once a year. Of course in the midst of these two projects she shuttled Anthony and Edward to baseball and soccer practice.

With so much going on it was no surprise that they missed church the following Sunday. Robert was at the office all day laboring over the details of the report, while April once again chauffeured the boys to their games.

The third Monday when Robert pulled out of his driveway on his way to work he noticed something that disturbed him. His neighbor across the street was an older man and his wife. They hadn't had time to get to know them that well but they seemed to be nice enough. There was a large oak tree in the neighbor's front yard and it shaded the lawn so much that that their Bermuda grass had died leaving the yard pretty barren. He had seen the neighbor out there one afternoon and walked over to say hello and see what the old man was doing. Apparently the HOA had written them a letter about their lawn and said they would have to plant new grass. So he was spreading fescue seed in the lawn and had been told that it would do well in the shade.

Now when Robert looked at it he could see that other plants were also doing well. The yard was full of weeds. There were dozens of milkweed plants, dandelions, chickweed, crabgrass and clover. These were doing so well that the grass could barely be seen. The weeds had crowded out the fescue and he saw only a spot or two of actual grass and no doubt the weeds would soon take those spots over as well. Robert just shook his head. They lived in an exclusive development for a reason. He hoped that the HOA would notify the couple soon that this was unacceptable.

He didn't want to report them, but he would if this wasn't corrected soon.

The week turned out to be just as busy as or even busier than the previous two. That Saturday night they again had a late dinner. This time it was hamburgers and fries with milkshakes from a fast food place near their home. Munching on his food Anthony suddenly looked at them and said, "Hey I thought we were going to start going to church on Sunday. Are we going tomorrow?"

Robert looked at April and answered, "Well we've just been so busy every week, son. And tomorrow you have a game at 9:00 and Edward has one at 11:00. Do you want to skip those?"

Anthony looked at Edward and they both looked down at the floor. "Well, no the team is depending on me" said Anthony. "And Edward's team might be a man short without him."

"See that's the problem. And it's not just you guys. I'm going through a very hectic time at work and mom is so busy right now she can barely get you two to your games in between her other projects. I'm afraid we're all just too busy."

After they boys had showered and gone to bed April said, "It is a shame we can't make time for church. I think we all enjoyed it."

"I know and I agree. It's just not a good time. There's too much going on. Maybe things will settle down after a while and we'll be able to get started. We'll get everything organized and together and then we can start church and follow Christ like we want to do."

Of course life didn't settle down. It stayed busy and so did Robert and his family.

# Chapter Nine

Jason had hugged and kissed Grandma Ruth when they met on the parking lot and now he walked along beside her and let her hold his arm as they entered the building. Emily was right behind them, walking along with her mother-in-law. Like everyone else he was amazed at the reception and at first he suspected that she had announced the week before that her family would be attending this week with her. But it soon became apparent that this was just the normal reception she received each week. He could understand why. Grandma Ruth was the sweetest person he had ever known and she was someone who simply exuded goodness. She had always been steadfast in her faith and it was obvious that she was not just loved but highly respected by the people in her church.

Like Ethan, Robert and Violet, Jason had many memories of the church as he walked through the hall and into the sanctuary. He had gone to the same VBS sessions and remembered hearing bible stories and playing games. He had not attended Sunday School as long as the others. When his siblings grew older and could stay home alone on Sunday they, mostly Violet if truth be known, were given the responsibility of taking care of him as well. Still, he had fond memories of the few years he did attend. He had also been married in this sanctuary.

Now as he sat in the pew listening to the sermon and holding Emily's hand he felt himself being strangely drawn into the words. Taking in the words and the meaning of the message he realized, maybe for the first time, that church was more than just a place to bring kids and give them structure and moral understanding. It applied to everyone. Everything this pastor was saying seemed to make sense and it was as if the words were aimed directly at him. He knew he was a pretty good person all things considered, but he had at times sensed a lack of direction, a lack of purpose, a sense of being unfulfilled. Now he had to consider that this might be due to a lack of God in his life. If there was a God, and he believed there was, then he was separated from him. He was not in communion with that God. When the pastor brought the service to a close and they were praying, he prayed for the first time ever as an adult and simply asked God that if He was really there to please show him the way, show him the next steps to take. When he finished he felt Emily tug at his hand and realized how hard he had been squeezing hers as he prayed.

They followed the others to lunch at the restaurant and on the way he asked Emily, "So what did you think of the service?"

"You know, I have to say I was deeply moved by some of the things that I heard. It was very thought provoking."

"I thought so too. I've always thought that when our family came along we would start going somewhere, but now I'm wondering if we should start sooner than that."

"I wouldn't mind looking into that. This church is too far away though. It's worse than your commute every day, but there are a number of churches closer to home and we could visit some."

"Let's think about that. I definitely want one where we feel like we fit in with everyone else."

When they arrived at the restaurant, Ethan and Robert and their spouses and children had already taken seats at the table as had Grandma Ruth and Elizabeth. Jason and Emily sat at the other end next to the children and across from each other. Soon afterward Violet arrived and sat at the foot of the table next to them. Before the food arrived Grandma Ruth stood and thanked everyone for attending. She encouraged them all to come again. The joy simply beamed in her face as she spoke to them.

He looked at each of his brothers and sister then and wondered what they were thinking. It was pretty obvious that Ethan was simply being polite and would not be seen in any church again soon. Robert however spoke about the service and seemed to have been affected by it. He nodded enthusiastically when Grandma Ruth invited them to come again and he told her that they had all really enjoyed it. Violet was even more effusive in her compliments about the service. As things quieted down she told Jason and Emily that she had really been moved and was planning to make some changes in her life. Jason had always been especially fond of his big sister and knew that change would definitely be good for her. He hoped she would follow through. He told her that he and Emily were thinking the same thing and planned to visit some churches closer to their home.

When the meal was over he walked out with Grandma Ruth and told her what Emily and he were thinking. She listened and nodded approvingly. "I think that sounds wonderful, Jason. I'll be praying that you two find the right church home."

They then drove back to their place. Winding along the county road leading to their house, Jason noticed that the farmers were starting to prepare their fields for planting. The fields were freshly plowed and furrows dug. Seeds would soon be in the ground. He always marveled at how a tiny seed, whether it was a flower or corn or whatever, could grow into a seedling and then a mature plant and finally produce its own fruit. Even though they did no farming themselves he always enjoyed seeing the process play out each spring and summer as he drove to and from work. It really was its own kind of miracle.

Pulling into their driveway Emily said, "Okay, Mister. I'm going to hold you to the plan. This week let's think about and notice the churches around here and make a list of the ones we want to visit. What do you say?"

"I say you're a hard taskmaster. No, really though I think that's a great idea. Your job is closer to home than mine so you might ask some people at work or some customers where they go. That might give us some ideas."

"I can do that."

"Okay then, let the search begin" he stated and they both laughed as they held hands and walked into their house.

## Chapter Ten

Over the next three weekends Jason and Emily visited three different churches. The first one was very traditional. The men all wore suits and ties and the ladies had on their Sunday best. They were greeted warmly when they first entered the building but then only a few people acknowledged them with a handshake and greeting. The music was also traditional with hymns and a choir, and the message was sound and on point. They couldn't say anything was really wrong with the church, but they weren't sure they would ever quite feel at home there.

Their next choice was in stark contrast to the first one. They were greeted enthusiastically by everyone they met. In fact enthusiasm could describe the entire experience. The songs again were traditional hymns but they were led by a praise team of four singers and they were accompanied by occasional shouts and hallelujahs from the congregation. It reminded Jason of some rock concerts he had attended in the past. The pastor delivered a message with vibrato voice that went from shouts to whispers and tenor to bass with each point he made. It was sometimes difficult to even hear a complete sentence, especially with members of the audience shrieking and shouting their praise. A lady in the back started speaking in tongues as the pastor reached the climax of his sermon.

When they got in their car to leave Jason looked at Emily and said, "Wow! What did you think of that?"

"That was all new to me! I've heard of speaking in tongues and all the shouting but that's my first time to see it."

"What I heard of the message seemed to be okay, and I don't doubt their beliefs or their enthusiasm but I don't think it's my type of service."

"Totally agree, big guy. Let's go somewhere to eat and replenish ourselves. That wore me out" Emily laughed.

The following Sunday they attended a church that one of Emily's customers had suggested. It was actually a little closer to home than the first two and judging by the number of cars in the parking lot, it had about the same number of attendees as their first choice. Again, they were welcomed warmly when they walked in and then several people greeted them as they found their way to the auditorium. They had a coffee stand with some pastries just outside the auditorium and Jason noticed that people were taking their cups into the service. Jason loved his coffee so this was definitely a good sign. Once inside they found that instead of a choir or praise team this church had a band and two singers. The band consisted of two guitars, rhythm and lead, a bass, drummer and keyboard. He wasn't familiar with the songs they did but he really liked the music. He noticed that Emily was really into the music as well. The words were displayed on a large screen so they mouthed the lyrics as the music played. After two songs they had a prayer and then everyone turned and greeted each other before sitting down. The sermon was part of a series that was dealing with how to live a separated life for Christ and still be able to function in a world that seemed to turn more and more away from Christianity. Fortunately it was the first message in the series and so they were not missing anything from previous sermons. The service ended with one more song and then they were greeted again by several people as they made their exit.

"You know, I think that's the one. I really felt at home there. I wouldn't mind hearing some of the older hymns but I did like the more modern music" Jason said.

"Ah, you just liked having coffee while you sung and listened" Emily teased. Then she added, "But seriously that's the first time I've felt right too."

They attended there again the next Sunday and met the pastor, Dr. Gerald Freeman. He was very friendly and although he hadn't met them that first Sunday he recognized them as having visited. Soon afterward they decided to make it official and join the church. They attended a two-Sunday class for new members that explained the organization and beliefs of the church. Then both Jason and Emily were baptized. For that they invited the family but only Grandma Ruth and his mother Elizabeth showed up. They were both overjoyed and Grandma Ruth told Jason that her prayers had been answered.

The more they attended the more they fell in love with the church and its people. More importantly their understanding and love for Jesus grew beyond anything they would have imagined. Jason was overflowing with enthusiasm and began sharing his experience with others at work when the opportunity arose. He was careful not to come off as preachy or like some holier than thou bible thumper. He was just a regular guy whose life had truly been changed because of his faith. Most of the people he encountered lived too far away to attend his church, but he encouraged them to find one that was true to the Bible and where they felt welcome and comfortable. He was thrilled when some of his coworkers actually followed his lead and accepted Christ as well. Emily was equally excited about their new discovery and told people at her work and her customers about it when the opportunity presented itself. Working closer to home she was blessed to see some of those she spoke with come to their church and become active there.

Driving home one Sunday after church Jason couldn't help but notice that the corn was now five or six feet high and had fresh corn cobs hanging from the plants. It was ready to harvest. He stilled marveled at how the field had been just freshly plowed soil not that long ago and now the seeds had grown and produced a crop. Looking at Emily he said, "Dr. Freeman asked me today if I would consider working with the youth group. I told him I didn't think I knew the bible well enough yet, but he said I didn't have to teach. That might come later, but for now they just need some assistants to be there and help as needed. I'm thinking I might do it."

"I think you should. I've been thinking of helping in the nursery. They're always saying they need help and I think I would enjoy it."

"Hey you could learn to change a diaper, so you'll know how when our kids come along" he laughed and she just smiled and shook her head.

A few months later they agreed to meet Grandma Ruth and Elizabeth for lunch one Saturday. It was good to get together with them again. Grandma Ruth asked about their church and they updated both of them about the church and their own growth as Christians.

"I just wish that Ethan and Robert and Violet could find a place and get involved" Jason said. "I've tried talking to them but it doesn't seem to do any good."

Grandma Ruth nodded sadly. "I know. Robert and Violet seemed to enjoy the service on my birthday so much. They were so excited, so hopeful. But you see really believing in God and really accepting Christ into your life is more than an emotional, joyful hearing of the gospel; someone truly saved will persevere and live a life that shows it. They had an emotional response that day, but you and Emily have really been changed. I'm so thankful for that."

"I hope they will follow suit someday Grandma".

"So do I Jason. I pray for it every day."

# Epilogue

This story was based on the parable of the sower. The parable of the sower is one of the most told parables being found in the gospels of Matthew (13:3-23), Mark (4:3-20) and Luke (8:4-15). After telling the parable to the crowd Jesus takes time to explain the meaning to his disciples.

The sower is one who spreads the message of the gospel, which is represented by the seed. The soil describes different conditions of the human heart and how it receives that message.

Some of the soil falls on hard ground by the roadside and will never take root. This portrays the person (Ethan) who is hardened by sin and he hears the gospel but doesn't understand it; Satan, represented by the birds, snatches it from his heart and it never takes root. They hear the Word but it never really permeates their soul.

Other seed falls on rocky ground. This is the person (Violet) who hears the Word and immediately receives it with joy, but they have no firm root in themselves and quickly fall away when affliction or persecution or temptation comes their way.

Still other seed falls onto ground crowded with thorns and weeds. This describes the person (Robert) who hears the Word but the concern for money and the worries of this world consume him and he becomes unfruitful. He says "Let me get my life together and then I will follow Christ".

Gladly some of the seed falls on good, fertile soil as represented by Jason and Emily. This is the person who hears and understands the word. This person matures in their faith and bears fruit. As stated by Grandma Ruth salvation is more than an emotional, joyful hearing of the gospel; someone truly saved will persevere and live a life that shows it.

# Like a Fox

*by*
*Bobby J Watson*

*"Be wise enough to learn from the past, shrewd enough to capitalize on the present, and clever enough to prepare for the future."*

*– Matshona Dhliwayo*

# Chapter One

"He's expecting you" the receptionist said as Marcus arrived at the office of his boss Antonio. He had worked for this man for several years and met with him numerous times each week, so this meeting was nothing out of the ordinary. Marcus was the Executive Vice President of the holding company that Antonio owned and in many ways he was more the hands-on leader of the company than his boss. The holding company consisted of a loan company where the borrower gave the company title to their car in return for a high-interest loan. A number of check-cashing companies were also part of the group, as was a bank that made business loans to corporate customers. These were generally businessmen who, for various reasons, couldn't get loans at traditional banks.

Marcus entered the lavish office which housed an expansive oak desk that was large enough to serve as a ping-pong table. Behind it was an equally large and cushiony leather chair. In front of the desk were two straight-backed chairs that were more designed to facilitate short visits than comfort. Marcus took a seat in one of these and waited while Antonio finished a phone call. Antonio was a tall, stoutly built man with a ruddy complexion in his mid-fifties. He had jet black hair that was starting to show a few gray streaks. He also carried an aura of darkness that gave you the distinct impression that he was not a man to be taken lightly. If the term "godfather" came to mind, it would be perfectly reasonable.

Those who knew the inner workings of his business knew that the loan office, the bank, and the check-cashing companies, while profitable enough on their own, largely served as money laundering fronts for associates of Antonio who were connected to drug cartels and gun running operations. No one knew these inner workings better than Marcus. Antonio hung up the phone and looked at Marcus and asked "Marcus, how long you been with me?"

Marcus didn't care for the tone of the question and wondered where this was going. "Twelve, thirteen years."

"I been good to you?"

Now Marcus was getting more concerned. He knew Antonio was not a man to be trifled with. "More than good."

"I think so too. You've been like a son or a little brother to me. That's why I'm surprised that someone has told me that you've been mishandling my business."

"What! Who told you that lie, Antonio? I've never done you wrong." Actually he had and he wondered who had fed this to his boss.

"Doesn't matter. I want you to bring the books in tomorrow morning. And I want everything. You understand?"

"Sure, sure. And when you see everything's okay, I want whoever told you this taken care of."

"We'll see. And Marcus, I love you like my own son. If I found anyone else cheating me, they'd be done for, but you'll just be out on the street and on your own. Of course if you ever talked, well then I'd have to take care of you like anyone else."

Marcus left the office and went into the restroom in the hallway. He felt flushed and short of breath. He turned on the tap water and splashed his face to cool down. He tried to regulate his breath as he grabbed some paper towels and dried himself. He couldn't believe this was happening. He knew that he had lost Antonio's confidence and was almost certainly out of a job tomorrow. When Antonio reviewed the books tomorrow he would know that Marcus had been keeping part of the profits for himself and even charging excess fees that he pocketed. He had been doing this for years without anyone suspecting it, but now someone had gotten on to his scheme. He couldn't possibly change the books enough by tomorrow morning to cover it up. His goose was cooked. He needed a Plan B.

He went to the parking lot and got into his BMW M3 Sedan and drummed on the steering wheel as he tried to come up with something. He then drove to his apartment and collapsed on the sofa. He couldn't go to some legitimate corporate job and start over. That would require a lower salary than he had gotten accustomed to and he couldn't step back in his lifestyle. He had spent his excess graft instead of investing it, so he couldn't live off his investments either. No, he needed a way to maintain his current level of income after Antonio fired him. What could he do?

Marcus sat and pondered his dilemma for another hour with different ideas running through his head. He even considered going to the FBI and becoming an informant, going into witness protection with a guaranteed income, and testifying against Antonio and his cronies. No, he couldn't do that to his boss and if he did there was no guarantee that they wouldn't find him eventually and make an example out of him. No, that wouldn't work.

Finally, he hit on what he thought might be a plan. He knew all of the corporate customers who had taken out bank loans for substantial sums. Indeed he had made a nice amount of money on some of these loans by charging additional "processing" fees and padding his own wallet. He also knew several customers who had corporate checking accounts at the bank that were actually just conduits to launder money. Yes, he knew more than a few dirty little secrets that gave him some influence with these people. Perhaps they would be willing to listen to a proposition from him that would benefit both parties.

He then made a list of the ones that he thought would be most likely to listen to his proposals. It was now nearly noon and he would need to act quickly. Tomorrow morning didn't leave much time and he needed to have these deals in place by then. Always a detailed planner, Marcus looked up the address of each location and planned a route that would be the most efficient. He thought about calling ahead but he couldn't risk being put off till a later time. He decided that showing up unexpectedly would catch the people off guard and give him the advantage of surprise.

Getting in the BMW and driving toward the first location, he said to himself "Okay Antonio you think you've caught the fox guarding the henhouse, but don't forget that this ole boy is smart like a fox too."

# Chapter Two

Joshua and his wife Sharon were sitting in their living room. Sharon was always busy with one of her crafts: knitting, sewing, tatting. She was quite skillful and found these hobbies relaxing. If not engaged in them she might be reading or working on an occasional dot-to-dot picture book. Joshua was mostly a reader although he also enjoyed an occasional sporting event on television. Tonight, as every night around 7:00 PM, he was reading a chapter or two of scripture. Closing his bible, he looked over at Sharon who was busy knitting and said, "I was just reading in Matthew Chapter 19 about that rich young ruler. You know the one. He said he had kept all the commandments and wanted to know what else he needed to do to inherit eternal life. Jesus told him to sell his possessions and give the money to the poor and then follow him. But he refused because he was wealthy and couldn't give up everything."

"Sure, I remember that one. Kind of sad, huh?"

"Yes, but it reminded me of something that's kind of been bothering me."

"Uh oh, I hope you don't want to sell everything and move to a monastery or something" she joked.

"No, not that drastic but I have been thinking that we could probably do more with what we have. God has really blessed us and sometimes I just think we don't do enough with what he's given us. I'm confident of our salvation; we have both trusted Jesus for that, but it just seems we could do more to help out the church or other ministries that are trying to reach people."

"Okay, I see. Do you have anything specific in mind?"

"No, it's just kind of a nagging feeling that I've had for quite a while now. I guess I've kind of been afraid to bring it up. I don't want you to misunderstand."

"I think I understand and if you really think this is something God wants us to do then you need to pursue it. Why don't you set up a meeting with Pastor Paul and run it by him. See what he thinks. He may be able to give you some ideas, and it definitely wouldn't hurt to discuss your feelings with someone else."

"Discuss my feelings? Come on Sharon, you know us men don't do that. We're no good with feelings" he laughed.

"True, we do all know that" She giggled.

"But yeah, seriously I think that's a good idea. I'll try to set up a meeting with him. You want to come?"

"No, I think just you and him and then we can discuss any ideas you come away with. All I ask is that whatever we do, let's make sure we're both okay with it."

"Absolutely" he replied.

Pastor Paul was not the senior pastor at their church. He was an associate pastor, but he and Joshua had a good relationship. Both men were in their late forties and had grown children who were married. Joshua had two grandchildren, while Paul was not yet a grandparent. Paul had led a number of bible studies that Joshua had attended and he appreciated the pastor's insights on scripture. They had engaged in numerous friendly conversations over the years and Joshua had gained a great deal of respect for the man. He called the church office the next day and arranged to meet for coffee on Saturday morning.

They met at a small coffee shop that's centrally located between their two homes. Paul ordered a Danish and black coffee. Joshua countered with a bear claw and black coffee. Noting that they both ordered black coffee, they laughed that neither of them was into the flavored coffees and lattes that are so popular these days. And they agreed that coffee should be hot and not iced. Then after exchanging updates about their families, they got down to the more serious business. Joshua explained the thoughts that he had been having while Paul quietly but thoughtfully listened, nodding his head on occasion.

Wrapping up, Joshua said "And Paul I'm not doing this because I'm worried about my salvation. I know that we don't earn our salvation. I've trusted Christ for that and I'm secure in my faith but I just believe I could be doing more."

"Well I'm glad you said that and you know that I agree with you. But you also know that Jesus more than once encouraged his followers to store up treasure in heaven. We don't know exactly what rewards are waiting for us there, beyond eternal life, but I think we often ignore the importance he put on building up your heavenly treasure rather than your earthly one. There has to be a good reason for that."

"Sharon's afraid I'm going to sell everything, start wearing sackcloth and move us to a monastery. But I'm not talking about living in poverty. I just think if we're wise with what God has given us that most of us can do a lot more that we choose to do. We plan and work hard to make money for what we need but maybe we should be just as concerned with how to use it for spiritual things. After all, we say it all belongs to him."

Paul nodded and addressed Joshua by his more common moniker, "you know Josh I guess each person has to decide how much they can give up. He does call some to give up everything like that rich young ruler, but I don't think he expects or requires that from all of us. But like you said, most of us can do more than we choose."

Paul then filled Joshua in on a number of projects and missions the church was involved in such as supporting an orphanage in Guatemala and sponsoring a food pantry in their own community. He pointed out that there were other worthwhile missions administered by charitable organizations and mentioned some specific ones to Joshua. Joshua wasn't yet sure which ones he felt drawn to, but he left believing that they should increase their support and involvement in some of these causes.

He went home and recapped the meeting for Sharon who listened intently and asked occasional questions to clarify what was said. After this they did something that was a bit unusual for them. They knelt in front of their sofa and prayed that God would guide them and show them what their next steps should be.

Standing up Sharon said, "You know Josh I think you've got us on the right track. I can't wait to see how God answers our prayer."

# Chapter Three

Marcus pulled into the parking lot of the strip center and sat for a moment. He ran the conversation he was about to have through his mind and then nodded his head and slapped the steering wheel. Yes! He knew what he was going to say. The strip center was typical of many in the city with a café that served breakfast and lunch, a small book store specializing in new and classic comic books, a donut shop and the ever present dry cleaners. Next to the dry cleaner on one end of the center was the Cash Now Pawn Shop. Marcus walked into the pawn shop and noticed that there were two customers browsing and one young man behind the counter. His name tag said Jonah.

"Hi Jonah, I'm Marcus and I'm here to see Mr. Dillan. I saw his car in the parking lot so I know that he's here. Don't worry, he knows me."

The young man went through a door behind the counter and came back a minute later. He just motioned for Marcus to enter the same door and then resumed his position at the counter. Marcus walked through the door and across a small entry way to the office of Barry Dillan who owned the pawn shop. The office was surprisingly large and lavish with a large desk centered against the rear wall. One side wall was covered with several oil paintings of landscapes, while the opposite wall was covered with an equally impressive number of framed photographs of sports figures ranging from baseball to football to hockey and basketball stars. Marcus had been in the office a few times prior to this and always wondered if Barry had purchased these or if they had been pawned at one time or another.

Barry was in his mid-forties and stood about 5'9". He was neither heavy nor thin and would have been a pretty average looking guy except for his distinct mustache and goatee. They were both brown, matching his wavy head of hair. The other thing you noticed immediately was his intense green eyes. He always reminded Marcus of a cheating gambler in one of those old western movies or the snake oil salesman hawking a magic elixir. Like one of those characters, he always had a cigarette dangling in his mouth. He now stood and greeted Marcus with a handshake and said, "Marcus, my friend. I wasn't expecting you."

"Sorry to drop by without calling first, but I really needed to see you this afternoon."

"Well if it's about my payment I know it's a few days late but I plan on making it soon."

"How would you like to have it forgiven entirely?"

"Whoa! That would be great but what's the catch?"

What was the catch indeed? Barry had three pawn shops in town and made what would have been a good living for most people from them. But unfortunately Barry had a bad habit. He loved to gamble and he wasn't very good at it. Several times a year he flew to Las Vegas to try his hand at the casinos. He also followed horse racing and attended the Kentucky Derby, The Preakness and Belmont Stakes every year. He prided himself on knowing horses but this seldom was evident in his choices for winners. To cap things off he was a prolific bettor on sporting events and proved no better at that than he did with the horse races.

To keep his head above water he did two things. He quietly made it known around the area that he was open to accepting stolen goods, thus serving as a fence for thieves who specialized in high-end merchandise. He also was a regular borrower from the bank. Both Antonio and Marcus knew the source of much of his money and so he paid a premium rate of interests for these loans. In addition to that Marcus slapped on an extra percentage point and a processing fee that added to the amount due. Of course he pocketed this excess.

"No catch. Just a proposition."

"Oh, a proposition" laughed Barry. "And what's that?"

"I'm going to be looking for a new job soon and I think I could really benefit you by acting as a consultant to your business. Let's be honest Barry, outside of this shop you're not much of a businessman. I know investments and other opportunities much better than you do, and I can make you a lot of money. In return I would just want a modest regular salary and a bonus percentage based on the profit I earn for you."

"Well, that is interesting. Are you in some kind of trouble with Antonio? And other than forgiving my late payment, what do I get in return?"

"Let's just say that Antonio and I have some differences of opinion. Here's what I can do. I can eliminate the processing fee and a point of your interest on future payments. I can also take what you've paid for those two things over the years and apply them to the principal you owe. That will eliminate a substantial amount of your balance due. We can have that loan paid off entirely within a year. How does that sound?"

"Sounds to me like I've been paying more than I was supposed to for all these years."

"That may be true, but it doesn't matter now. What do you say?"

"You sure you can do this and Antonio won't be the wiser? I don't want any trouble with that guy. People who get sideways with him don't end up too good."

"You agree to our deal right now today and I guarantee you that I can fix it where he never knows."

Barry spun around in his chair to face the back wall and stared at it for a minute. When he swiveled back to face Marcus he said, "Alright, if you can really do this without him knowing then I'm in. Now tell me what you consider a modest salary and how that percentage bonus would work."

They discussed the numbers for several minutes and agreed on figures that both believed they could live with and then both men stood and shook hands. Barry walked around and showed Marcus out of his office.

Getting in his BMW Marcus thought about the deal. The numbers didn't replace what he had been making, but if he could get a couple of similar deals in place, then he would be positioned to maintain his lifestyle. With that in mind he started the engine and began driving to the office of Harry Hindman, a building contractor who could benefit greatly from his services.

## Chapter Four

One of the charitable organizations that Paul had mentioned to Josh was a shelter that served hot meals to homeless people. It was not associated with their church and so he wanted a chance to see it for himself and learn more about it. Sharon was a whiz with researching things on the computer and she delved into the finances of the organization to see just how their money was being spent. If someone worked there full time she understood that they deserved to be paid, but she also wanted to make sure it wasn't an exorbitant amount. Too many so-called charities used their status to pay huge salaries to the management. She learned that they only had two paid workers. One was the director who managed the donations and worked with area restaurants and grocery stores to help supply the food needed for the operation. He made a modest salary that seemed reasonable. The other person was a head cook and server who made slightly less than the manager. Unpaid volunteers made up the rest of the labor force. She found no expenses that seemed out of line and determined that 86% of their donations were spent on food and shelter, including the purchase of single beds, sheets, and blankets.

Josh stopped by the shelter one day after work the week following his conversation with Pastor Paul. He arrived about thirty minutes before they started the evening meal which that day consisted of beef stew, cornbread and coffee or tea to drink. A bakery had also donated some layer cakes that were due to expire the next day. He asked one of the volunteers who was setting out dishes and utensils where the manager could be found and she pointed him to a man in his late fifties or early sixties who was speaking with the cook. He went over and introduced himself and the man, whose name was James Snow, greeted him with a smile and a handshake. He told Josh that they normally fed an average of seventy five people a meal and they served breakfast and dinner. He explained that one of their challenges was being able to provide fresh vegetables and fruits. Stores only donated these when they were expiring and sometimes they went bad because they couldn't use them quickly enough or they didn't have adequate cold storage. Their other big need was more shelter space. They only had twenty beds and these were taken quickly, especially on hot and cold days and nights. There was a space for lease across the street. It had been a clothing store but had closed and moved to the suburbs. It would enable them to set up fifty or more additional beds but they couldn't afford the asking price for the lease.

He invited Josh to stay and help serve dinner but Josh declined, saying he needed to speak with his wife and that they might return to help in the future.

He arrived home a few minutes later than usual and found that Sharon had prepared pot roast, mashed potatoes, and asparagus for dinner. For dessert she had baked a delicious red velvet cake. As he enjoyed the meal and told her about his visit to the shelter, he couldn't help but think about the people there who were having stew and cornbread for dinner. Not that anything was wrong with stew and cornbread but it was quite a contrast to what he and Sharon were eating. Tonight at the shelter they also had cake, but he understood that was not always the case.

After recapping his conversation with James Snow, Sharon filled him in on what she had found. She was actually pretty impressed with how the financial side of the mission was being handled and felt sure that anything they donated would be put to good use. She concluded with "so what do you think our next step should be?"

"You know, I liked everything I saw but I think it would be a good idea to volunteer a night or two and see what our impression is after working with the people and seeing what it's really like."

"That makes sense and I thought you might say that. So I got GPS directions so that I could drive down and meet you there after work one day."

"Ha-ha! Anticipating me, huh? Well, okay let's just do it tomorrow evening then."

They finished the rest of their meal in thoughtful silence. The red velvet cake was delicious.

The next day they met at the shelter as they agreed. Josh had time to introduce Sharon to James and to Theodore the cook before they were given a quick lesson in how to serve the food. Tonight was mashed potatoes, pinto beans and a hamburger patty. The volunteer who was giving instructions said the main thing was to politely decline any requests for additional amounts or second helpings. After everyone was served and a cutoff time had been reached, then any leftover food could be given on a first-come first-served basis. While they were listening to these instructions some of the homeless started coming in and forming a line. Sharon noticed that some were quite dirty and had very worn and torn clothing, while others looked cleaner and were better dressed. These were the more newly homeless who had not seen the wear and tear of the weather the others had endured.

As they were serving a few did indeed ask for additional food and it was difficult to say no to them, but most seemed to know the rules and expressed their thanks when served. Just as with the clothes you could tell those who had been in this line many times and those who were new. Most of the newer ones were unsure of themselves and were obviously embarrassed by their situation. Most of them said nothing, but a few quickly explained that they had recently lost jobs and were evicted from their apartments or homes and hoped to be employed again soon. Like many people they lived paycheck to paycheck and unemployment checks had either ended for them or were simply not enough to meet basic needs. Others were dealing with addictions and had lost everything including the support of their families. Josh and Sharon learned quickly that the reasons for their current situation varied greatly, but they all had two things in common. They were hungry and they were homeless.

They each drove their own car home and so didn't have a chance to talk until they arrived there. They agreed it had been a moving experience and both of them felt it was something worthy of their continued support. Then Sharon broached another subject.

"The realtor called today. She has a home in Pinnacle Acres that she wants us to visit. She says it sits on a half-acre of land, has a pool and is exactly what we've been wanting."

"Oh boy. You know, Sharon, I've been thinking about that and you may not like what I've been thinking."

"Spit it out, big boy" she said playfully.

"Well, I'm just not sure we really need another house and certainly not a bigger one. This place has more room than we need and it even has spare bedrooms for when my brother or your sister visit with their families. We've kept the house well-maintained and this is about as safe as any neighborhood in the city. As for a pool, we have the community pool when we want to use it. And we'll have this house paid for by the middle of next year. Then the payment goes away and we only owe house insurance and property tax every year. Why start a new mortgage with higher payments? And here's the kicker. The money we save by staying here, we could use to help support things like the shelter. I don't want to sound all pious, but if we really believe it's God's money why not use it for his work?"

"I hate it when you make sense like that" she said, but he could see she was teasing him with that statement. "Pinnacle Acres is the most prestigious place to live in this city. It shows that we've really made it."

He nodded, trying to be understanding. He knew it had been her dream for a long time.

"But I've been thinking too" she continued. "I've actually been thinking the same things you have, especially after reviewing their finances and now seeing it for myself. So I agree with everything you've said and I think that's what we should do. I also think you owe me big time" she concluded with a giggle.

Following what they knew was God's calling Josh and Sharon started volunteering three nights a week at the shelter and soon knew almost every person they served by name. They also contributed fresh vegetables and fruit once a week and purchased two refrigerators for additional storage. When their mortgage was paid off they applied the amount that had been their house payment to leasing a space down the street from the shelter. This new space accommodated another sixty beds.

They often reminded each other that what they were doing here gave them more pleasure than Pinnacle Acres would ever have provided.

## Chapter Five

Marcus thought about Harry Hindman as he drove to the man's office. Hindman was a building contractor with a sketchy reputation. He had developed two subdivisions in the area within the last four years and had borrowed heavily from the bank to complete those projects. The homes were a blend of nice upper middle income homes and some that were definitely more upscale. They ranged in size from roughly two thousand square feet to over five thousand. The larger homes also had pools, game rooms, offices and additional bedrooms. Marcus had visited some of the homes under construction as part of his due diligence in approving the loans. They seemed to be quite nice and well-built.

It was important to ensure the quality because earlier in Hindman's career he had specialized in commercial projects. His company had built a number of large office buildings in the downtown area and in the far north side of the city where there was a booming commercial presence. The trouble began when the parking garage in one of his buildings collapsed and inspections revealed that it had been built with sub-standard concrete. One lady had been seriously injured, but fortunately no one had died. This led to similar inspections of other Hindman projects and a number of those were found to have similar issues. Reinforcement columns and other corrections were required which threw the company into Chapter 11 Bankruptcy. Authorities could not prove intentional negligence and so no criminal charges were filed. The reorganized company came out of bankruptcy and made the transition to private residences. However Hindman was now anathema to the national banking institutions and to most local banks as well. This had eventually brought him to Antonio's bank.

There he was welcomed with open arms and high percentage rates for his loans. The rates of course were made even higher by Marcus's additional percentage rate and processing fees. It was either accept these terms or go out of business and Hindman had reluctantly agreed to the terms with a promise of better rates in the future if he remained loyal to the bank and made payments on time. Unfortunately for him, that time had not yet arrived.

Marcus took the elevator up to the fourteenth floor and entered Hindman's corporate office. He had been here a few times before over the years and the receptionist recognized him.

"Sir, I don't have you down for an appointment today. Is Mr. Hindman expecting you?"

"He is not, but this is somewhat of an emergency. Please tell him that I need to see him and it's urgent."

The receptionist went in the adjoining office and in a few seconds Harry Hindman came out with her. Hindman was a man in his mid-fifties of average height and weight. He had black hair on the sides of his head that he combed over in an attempt to cover the very evident bald spot on top.

"Marcus, this is a surprise. I don't really have time for unscheduled appointments. I have a number of meetings today."

"I understand Harry and I apologize, but I think you'll be pleased with my interrupting your day if we can just talk for a few minutes."

"Okay, but it has to be quick." Then turning to the receptionist he said, "Call Kendall and tell her that I will be with her in twenty minutes." Marcus recognized the name of the company's CFO.

"Yes sir."

"Come on in the office Marcus."

Harry's office made those of both Antonio and Barry look plain and unremarkable in comparison. The walls were lined with models of various building projects past and future. Above these replicas were large framed pictures of those same projects, including aerial views of the housing developments. Harry's desk was nothing short of ornate and seemed almost as big as a billiard table. Behind the desk was a large window providing a breathtaking view of the city skyline. Along one wall was a large oak conference table with eight chairs. Marcus sat in a chair in front of Harry's desk.

"Make it quick, Marcus. What can I do for you?"

"No Harry, this time it's what I can do for you."

He explained that he would be parting ways with Antonio in the near future and was planning to provide consulting services to some of the bank's better clients. He proposed the same deal that he had made with Barry. Harry would pay him a nice but reasonable monthly retainer and Marcus would offer investment and financial advice. In return he would receive a percentage bonus on the profits from that advice.

"And other than your expert advice, what do I get in return?" Harry asked sarcastically.

"Well Harry, I'm sure you recall that when you first came to us we promised you better terms in the future if you met certain conditions. I'm willing to offer you those terms before my departure from the bank."

"More specific."

"Sure. Right now you owe a little over a million dollars on your loans. I can reduce that balance to $750,000 and I can apply our lowest interest rate to future payments."

"You can do that? And it won't get reversed when you leave?"

"I guarantee it."

"And now the bigger question. How bad is your trouble with Antonio and how can I be sure he will be okay with all this? He's not someone I want trouble with."

"I have no trouble with Antonio" he lied. "I've simply reached a point where I want to get out and try some things on my own. Antonio has been very good to me and there's no animosity or threats on his part."

Harry nodded slowly. "Okay, I can't very well turn down an offer like you're suggesting. Between the reduced principal and the lower interest it could save me half a million dollars. And I've known you long enough to know that you're one smart cookie when it comes to making money. If you weren't then Antonio wouldn't have kept you around this long. So I'm going to say yes contingent on you doing what you say you'll do. When will you start?"

"I'll let you know for sure in a day or two, but probably next week sometime."

"Sounds good. Welcome aboard."

The two men stood and shook hands and then Harry rushed off to his meeting with Kendall.

Marcus went to the parking garage and began thinking about his next conversation. Corey might be a little more problematic than these first two, but he might have even more to gain from working with Marcus too. So far things had gone perfectly according to plan. If Corey was agreeable he would be all set for life after Antonio. But a long night awaited him in order to be totally prepared for his meeting with the boss tomorrow.

# Chapter Six

A former mayor had established the New Start Initiative after he left office. It was an organization that purchased older homes that needed repair and were being sold well below market value. Volunteers would then refurbish the home and it would be given to a homeless person who met certain criteria. The criteria included being free from addiction and being willing to attend and complete job training classes that the charity offered. Other considerations were marital status, number of children if any and the belief that the applicant was sincere in wanting to improve their situation. Many of those who applied were members of AA or Celebrate Recovery and they needed to have been free from their addiction for an extended time to receive serious consideration.

This was another organization that Pastor Paul had told Josh about during their discussions and after looking into it he and Sharon had decided to become involved in it. Josh was a good software engineer and project manager but he had absolutely no innate ability as a carpenter, electrician or any other skill needed for home repair. However he did have a fairly strong back and could follow directions so his volunteer work was a mix of loading and unloading material, and doing supervised carpentry work. He was a danger to himself and others when wielding a hammer when he first started, but he did slowly improve with practice to the point that he could drive nails consistently and without injury.

Sharon proved to be a master with a paint brush and helped with chores like hanging window shades and curtains. She also helped with the continual clean-up that jobs like this required, but her greatest skill was on the telephone. She was very effective in procuring building supplies and equipment from businesses who agreed to donate to the organization after listening to her explain their mission. She and Josh were overjoyed when they saw their first project come to completion. The refurbished house, a small frame three bedroom with one bath, looked like new when it was finished. And they were moved to tears when they, along with other volunteers, helped a veteran and his wife and two boys move into the house. The ex-Marine had served multiple tours in the Middle East and had suffered from drug addictions and PTSD. He had now been free from addiction for six months and his mental state had also improved greatly. He was training through the charity to be a welder. The joy on the family's faces was unforgettable as they moved in that day.

Soon after that Josh paid a visit to Colburn Sedgewick, his financial adviser. Colburn had been his advisor for several years and Josh and Sharon both trusted him without reservation. They had first discovered him when Josh left one employer and joined another one. He had guided them in rolling the 401(k) from that previous employer into an IRA. Since that time they had established a number of different accounts with him for various purposes ranging from emergency funds to college savings accounts for their children. They planned to soon open new accounts for their grandchildren, one of whom was two and the other had just celebrated his first birthday.

Normally Colburn would summon them to his office once or twice a year for routine reviews of their accounts and their situation to see if any changes were needed. On rare occasions they would make an appointment on their own. This was pretty much limited to large unexpected events that required them to withdraw money from the emergency fund. Last year a hailstorm had pummeled their roof to the point that it needed replacement. To save on the premium they had agreed to a two percent deductible which proved to be more than they could pay from their own bank accounts after the storm. So they had visited Colburn and determined the best stock to sell in order to raise the cash. Today however they had made an appointment for an entirely different reason.

Julie the receptionist greeted them when they entered the office and offered them water or coffee which they declined. Julie was one of those outgoing, always happy, personalities that inevitably caused everyone she met to smile. They visited with her briefly until Colburn emerged from his office and met them with a handshake.

"So how have you guys been doing?"

"Doing fine, Colburn. Yourself?"

"I'm doing well also and if I complained what good would it do?" he chuckled.

"Isn't that the truth?"

They settled into chairs in front of Colburn's desk. His desk was pretty simple with a couple of framed family pictures, a pen set and a computer monitor on it. The monitor was positioned where it would swivel so that both he and his clients could see it while discussing their investments.

"So what are we doing today? I've been looking at your accounts and they all look good. There's one or two stocks we might consider trading but other than that, you seem to be in good shape."

Sharon then spoke up and said "Well Colburn, this will take a little explaining and you should know that it's not a whim. It's something we've given a lot of thought to recently."

Sharon was just as knowledgeable, and maybe a little more so, about their investments than Josh and he was glad that she had taken the lead. She proceeded to tell their advisor about the New Start Initiative and their involvement in it.

Colburn listened intently while she spoke, nodding his head occasionally to indicate he was following and understood their commitment. When Sharon was finished he said, "I've heard good things about that program and I can see that you guys are really invested in it." He then smiled and said "No pun intended. So where do I come into this?"

Sharon looked at Josh who now took the lead and explained their plan. "Colburn, we have that one account that we created a few years ago thinking it would just be available if we needed funds for a new house, an unusual vacation like a world cruise when we retire, a really catastrophic illness, something like that. What we want to do is change that to more of an income-based account and send the profits from it to the New Start Initiative every three months or so. And no, we haven't gone nuts. We've thought this through."

"I understand what you're saying but are you really that committed to this cause?"

"Yes, we really are and let me assure you that we don't plan to go overboard with this. Colburn, I don't know if you're a religious person or not."

"I go to church pretty often."

"Well then maybe you'll understand. Sharon and I decided a few months ago that God has really blessed us and we needed to be better stewards of what he's given us. We really believe that everything, including our investments, is his and we should be giving part of it to help further his kingdom here on earth."

"I think that's admirable, Josh."

"When this first came up I promised Sharon that we would not sell everything and move to a mountaintop in Tibet and I'll make that same promise to you."

Colburn laughed and said "I'll take you at your word on that and I can see that this is something the two of you have discussed and agreed on. So, let's look at what's in that account and see how we can restructure it to do what you want."

## Chapter Seven

Of the three people he had targeted, Corey presented the biggest challenge to Marcus. Corey was a smart business man but in addition to that he was also the most dangerous in Marcus's mind. Other than Antonio, Corey was the one person that Marcus feared the most. But he also presented the opportunity to make the most money since he dealt in very large sums of cash.

Corey was to put it simply a drug kingpin. He had started as a teenager selling pot on the street and had graduated to more serious and more lucrative drugs. Before he was even out of high school he had started recruiting other kids and some adults to sell for him. He attended community college and got an associate's degree while still building his drug empire. He had a very sharp mind and a persuasive personality that enabled him to become a threat to the local cartel representatives. By age twenty five he had effectively driven them out of business by a combination of threats and murder for hire. Of course the cartels don't like to be pushed around and a gang war seemed on the horizon when Corey sought out the cartel leaders and reached an agreement with them. Supply him with their drugs and he would sell them and share the profits. He convinced them that this was a better deal than continued warfare and thus became a partner of the cartel.

To launder his illicit gain he established a number of shell companies that bought real estate, usually single-family homes, for cash and then quickly sold the same property. The proceeds from the sales were then deposited into Antonio's bank. This had proven a very efficient and difficult to trace method for laundering the drug money. Of course Antonio and Marcus both knew the real source of these transactions but in their quest for the all mighty dollar, they followed the old adage that discretion is the better part of valor. In fact a significant number of the bank's clients were engaged in similar activities.

Marcus parked his BMW in an open spot in front of one of Corey's companies named Integrity Real Estate where he knew that Corey maintained his office. He couldn't help but shake his head and smile as he considered the name of the company. Integrity was a word that could never be used to describe the owner of this business he thought to himself. He entered the building and asked to see Corey. The receptionist asked his name and disappeared only to return shortly and direct him to a corner office down the hallway.

Corey greeted him with a handshake and asked him to sit. This office was very understated and plain in comparison to the others he had seen today. The desk was not overly large or ornate. There was a simple brown bookcase behind the desk and a couple of landscape pictures on the wall. Corey was a big barrel-chested man with black wavy hair. His face was marked by an afternoon shadow that added to his dark aura. His eyes were piercing and seemed to burn right through you.

"So what's up? What brings you here?"

Marcus explained his situation just as he had with Harry and Barry. Unlike the other two men Corey didn't have any large loans outstanding at the bank, but he did have a revolving credit account that was used as needed to fund his payroll and other expenses when needed.

"One thing I can do for you" Marcus suggested "is lower the interest rate by a point off that account and drop the processing fee. But more importantly I can help you make more money than you're making today on these real estate deals. I have some alternative ways to invest that money that will accomplish the same purpose and make a nicer profit."

"So you've been stealing some of that interest and the 'processing fee'" he said while emphasizing the quote marks with his fingers. "I always suspected that."

"Well Corey, let's just say that's the past. Let's focus on the future."

"Okay tell me how you propose to make more money for me."

"I have several ideas but I'll share one of them with you now."

Marcus then outlined a plan to build a casino that he would help manage for Corey. This of course would be done under the banner of a new company and would involve a substantial investment up front. But it was a business that was flush with cash. Neither of them said, though both knew, that a cash business like this was perfect for money laundering.

Corey sat with the fingers of his hands laced together and the two index fingers touching his lips as he listened to Marcus's proposals. He thought for a minute after Marcus finished and then said, "I thought casinos were illegal in this state."

"They are of course. But we both know they're perfectly legal fifty miles from here across the state line."

"True. What keeps me from just doing this myself?"

"Not a thing. But the bank has some of those existing casinos as clients and I know quite a bit about their operation. I also know people who can manage and run them for us. And besides that, this is just one idea. I have others too that will make a lot of money for us, Corey."

"You keep saying us. We're not partners."

"Oh of course not. But I know you will compensate me well if I make a lot of dough for you."

They then discussed how that compensation would work and reached an agreement they both approved.

Corey stood up and put out his hand. Marcus shook it.

"So when do we start moving forward with this?"

"I'll take care of the interest rate and processing fee tomorrow and there will be some retroactive credit on it too. It will be a few days, maybe a week, before I can start on the rest of it. I have some things to clear up and take care of first. You'll hear from me soon."

"Alright. Sounds good. Let's make some money."

Marcus walked out to his car. He drove toward the bank but stopped at a local sports bar he sometimes frequented after work. Enjoying a vodka martini he thought about Corey. Of the three men Corey was the only one who hadn't asked about possible trouble with Antonio. He probably underestimated just how dangerous Antonio could be. Marcus hoped that he never had to find out.

Leaving the bar he entered the bank. All the employees were gone for the night just as he had hoped. The janitorial service was vacuuming and cleaning but that was okay. He went to his office and booted his computer. He had a lot of work to do before meeting with Antonio in the morning.

## Chapter Eight

Josh routinely retreated to his home office on Sunday afternoons to pay whatever bills were due in the coming days. Sundays were usually pretty quiet and restful days after they attended church services and he found it conducive to performing this mundane task, and sometimes doing a little financial planning at the same time. His office wasn't a man cave but it was decorated with pictures and other paraphernalia of his favorite sports teams. Sometimes after completing his business he enjoyed just sitting and reminiscing about some of the memories of those teams and his favorite players. Today though he ended his work and simply smiled and nodded his head with satisfaction.

He went downstairs and found Sharon reading a novel. She looked at him and said, "What? I know that look. What's made you so happy all of a sudden?"

"Well" he said, "I've got some good news. We just made the final payment on my car. It's all ours now."

"Oh, that's terrific. So when do we go car shopping?"

In the past they had always budgeted for a car payment. Each of them had a car and so they actually budgeted for two payments. Whenever they paid one off, they would immediately go car shopping for its replacement. They had figured that this way they had minimal car trouble, other than routine maintenance, and always drove one of the latest models.

"I've been thinking about that" Josh said.

"Uh oh, that can be dangerous" joked Sharon.

"Maybe so, but I've just been thinking that my car is still in great condition and has really low mileage. It actually could last me a few more years. Why not just keep it and apply that payment amount to some of the mission work being done by the church?"

"Wow! That's a curve ball, but it's something to think about. Then when my car is paid off in a few years, we could keep mine and buy you a new one. So we're always just making one payment at a time and the other going to missions."

"I hadn't thought that far ahead, but you're right. Gee, I like the way you think" he grinned and said.

"Before we take the plunge though, why don't you go talk with Pastor Paul again and get a better idea what missions they would use the money for?"

"That makes sense. We know the church is involved in a number of different things but we don't know the scope, the size or expense of each one. I'll try to set up an appointment with him sometime this week."

They met a few days later at the same small coffee shop they had met at before. Again Pastor Paul ordered black coffee and a Danish, while Josh stuck with black coffee and a bear claw. They laughed at their lack of creativity but Paul then said, "No it's not that we aren't creative. We're just consistent." They both laughed and agreed that was a more positive way to look at it.

Josh then explained what he and Sharon had in mind and why he had requested the meeting. When he finished Pastor Paul simply looked at him and shook his head from side to side. "Man, you guys are absolutely amazing" he said.

"We don't really think of ourselves that way. We really haven't cramped our lifestyle at all. We've just readjusted some of our priorities. When we work at the shelter or help refurbish the homes we feel like we're the ones being blessed, not the other way around."

"Commendable nonetheless" responded Paul.

He then explained in more detail some of the mission work of the church. They operated a clothing store that distributed free clothes and shoes to the homeless, but also to the working poor.

He explained that the clothes were good quality used clothes, but the shoes they provided were always new. "We always think about the homeless, but many people simply live on the edge from paycheck to paycheck and find it very difficult to afford new clothes. And good quality shoes and work boots in particular can be quite expensive."

"Another ministry we started recently is auto repair. You can't imagine how devastating it can be for the working poor when they have a major car expense. We have a handful of mechanics who volunteer their time to do the repairs, but the parts themselves can still be a major expense. We're very careful with this one. We want to help those who need help, but we don't want anyone taking unfair advantage of the service either."

"Another area is our youth. We have summer camps, but also retreats throughout the year and we see great success with these. We've baptized literally hundreds of kids over the years who have accepted Christ, but fees and supplies are an expense. Scholarships are always needed for summer camps and unfortunately we always have some young people who miss out because their parents simply can't afford it."

Josh was transfixed as he listened to this. He had always known the church had several extracurricular activities but now he was gaining a much deeper appreciation for it. Pastor Paul went on and explained several more mission activities to him, some of which he had heard about and others of which he had never been aware. When he finished Josh said, "Gosh, when I thought of missions in the past I just thought about trips to foreign countries but these are all local projects."

"We do also have some foreign missions and we work with other churches on those, but we feel that there are equally urgent needs right here at home."

Sharon was just as amazed when he went home and reported what he had learned to her.

"That's overwhelming" she said. "So which one would we donate to?"

"Talking to Pastor Paul, he suggested that we just give to the general mission fund and that way they can use the money where it's most needed. That makes sense to me if it does to you."

"Yes, based on what you've told me that does make sense." Then she looked at him and said "Okay, let's do it."

And so they did.

# Chapter Nine

Marcus sat at his desk staring through the plate glass window in the general vicinity of the janitorial crew. He wasn't really seeing them. He was lost in thought, considering where his office would be located by this time next week. He could probably find space in Harry's building or he could set up shop in Corey's place. Barry was more limited so that wasn't a choice. Or he could lease a place of his own. The more he thought about it that seemed like the better option. He didn't want any of his new clients to think he was more beholding or closer to one of them than the others. Besides he kind of liked the idea of planning and designing his own space. As he dreamt about what his new office would look like, he was startled by a loud banging noise. It was just a trash can that had been dropped by one of the crew onto the floor, but it awakened him from his reverie.

He then went into action on his laptop computer. It would take him a few hours to adjust the books to reflect these deals that he had made with Barry, Corey and Harry. Several correcting entries were required along with corresponding memo lines that explained the reason for the corrections. Antonio was no fool; the explanations would need to be reasonable and believable if he actually looked into the details. Marcus pounded away at the keyboard for three hours, occasionally stopping and reviewing his work to ensure it looked acceptable. He finally finished about 4:00 AM but then he had to print several reports that he would show Antonio during their meeting. He finished printing and gathered up the reports and after a final review, he felt he was ready for the meeting. It was now 5:30 in the morning.

Antonio usually arrived at the bank at 8:30 so Marcus drove to his apartment where he shaved, showered and changed into fresh clothes. He then went to a small café where he ordered two eggs over medium, bacon, wheat toast and orange juice for breakfast. He went over in his mind what he would say to Antonio as he gave him the reports. Finishing the orange juice, he drank a couple of cups of coffee with cream and sugar and then drove to the bank. He saw Antonio's car in his reserved parking spot and pulled in next to it.

Marcus sat down again in his own office and waited to be called into the meeting with Antonio. When the call came he picked up the reports and walked toward the corner office. He was nervous and a bit jittery, which was unusual for him, but he also felt a sense of confidence. He knew what he was going to say and he held out hope that Antonio would buy it all.

Antonio stood and shook his hand as he entered the office. "Good morning, Marcus."

"Good morning to you, sir. I hope you're doing well today."

After exchanging greetings he explained the various reports to Antonio who seemed to listen carefully and thoughtfully to each word. He then took the reports one at a time from Marcus and examined each of them, sometimes stopping to ask questions which Marcus quickly answered. When he had perused the last report he looked up at Marcus and said, "So, you've done all of this since yesterday. Very impressive, I must say."

"Oh, just printing these reports and getting them ready. They're all pretty standard reports as you know."

"No, I mean how you made all those adjusting entries to substantiate these reports and more impressively how you met with Harry, Corey, and Barry to cut deals with them and secure future work for yourself. I must say Marcus that you are without doubt the most cunning employee that I've ever had. Truth is you're almost as shrewd as yours truly. But did you really think those three would just accept what you said? All three called me after you left them to make sure that you were leaving here on good terms and I would be okay with you working with them."

"Oh my God, okay Antonio I give up. I guess my goose is cooked. So what's next? I mean, I'm sure that I'm fired."

LIKE A FOX

"No, Marcus. Not at all. I meant what I said. You are one shrewd cookie and I'd be the fool if I let someone with your talent go. There will definitely be some changes and you will be watched closely in the future, but you'll use that crafty mind of yours to help me and my businesses. I was truly impressed with what you did in such a short time and I am beyond intrigued at the casino idea you hatched with Corey. As a matter of fact I have set up a meeting with the three of us tomorrow to start that project."

Marcus walked back to his office and shut the door. He sat in his desk chair and swiveled it around to face the wall behind him. He was actually trembling a little bit as he contemplated what had just happened. Fear, anxiety, anger, joy, relief. Can you really experience all of those feelings at once? He sat there transfixed for several minutes before he turned back to his desk and took a deep breath. It sounded like he needed to start planning for a meeting tomorrow with Corey and Antonio. It should make a lot of money, just as he had told Corey.

As he went through the day his thoughts kept going back to the meeting with Antonio. He had escaped disaster. He had been handed a gift. His job and his life were intact and it seemed that Antonio had even more respect for him than before. The one thing that bound not just him and Antonio, but Harry, Barry, Corey and many of their other clients together was their love for money. They were definitely birds of a feather and they knew how to fly together.

# Chapter Ten

Josh and Sharon were sitting at home enjoying a quiet evening. She was reading a magazine article about gardening while he was browsing through news stories on his phone when it suddenly rang. Surprised to see that it was Pastor Paul, he clicked to answer the call. "Hello Josh, how are you and Sharon doing?"

"We're fine. Just sitting at home tonight."

"Well I should have called earlier but I had a couple of hospital visits to make. I was speaking with Pastor Stephen this afternoon and he asked that you and Sharon meet with him."

"Pastor Stephen?" Why would he want to see us?"

"Oh, don't worry. It's all good. When can you guys meet with him? I suspect the meeting will take about an hour."

Josh conferred with his spouse and then setup a time for the meeting with Paul. After wishing each other a good night and hanging up, he looked at Sharon with a quizzical expression. "Why would Pastor Stephen want to see us?"

Stephen was the senior pastor at their church and technically Paul's boss, although they worked more like colleagues. Josh and Sharon knew him and spoke to him each Sunday after services. But it was usually nothing more than a quick greeting and handshake. They had never interacted with him like they did with Paul. The church had a staff of five associate pastors, three administrative assistants and a media manager. Some of the pastors seldom preached but acted more as executive managers for the church. Stephen was a delegator and preached marvelous sermons, but he wasn't as hands-on with missions and other projects as the associate pastors. So getting a meeting request from him was unusual and really had Josh stumped. He had asked that Paul sit in on the meeting with them and Paul had readily agreed to do so.

Josh called his office the next morning and told them that something had come up and he would be a little late coming in to work. They then drove to the church and went inside. Vivien, one of the administrative assistants, had an office just inside the entry and she told them to go on up to Stephen's office. He was expecting them. A little nervous, Josh asked if Paul was already there and Vivien told him that Paul was on the way and would be there soon. They went up the elevator to Stephen's office. It was a nice, but understated, office with a couple of family pictures on his desk and an aerial view of the church grounds on one wall. Behind his desk Stephen had three large bookshelves that were crammed full with bibles, commentaries, histories and other Christian works. There was also a section that housed some of the classics like Moby Dick and War and Peace. Josh mused that he must be quite a reader. They had just greeted each other and settled into their chairs when Paul walked in and greeted everyone before taking his own seat.

Pastor Stephen began by saying "I was speaking with Paul yesterday and he filled me in on some of the things you two have done lately."

Trying to be funny and allay his nervousness Josh responded "Oh, I'm sure he exaggerated. We're not really that bad."

They all chuckled and Stephen continued. "No, I'm sure you're not, but seriously what you two have done during this past year is remarkable. You took funds you had targeted for a future home in Pinnacle Acres and instead used it to support a mission to feed the poor and lease space for additional beds. You directed one of your investment accounts toward the New Start Initiative and even help remodel the homes they buy and refurbish. And now I hear that you've paid off your car and have directed that payment amount each month to some of our own missions. Is all that correct?"

"Well yes sir, it is. We just became convinced that we should be using more of our resources to help grow the kingdom instead of just looking out for ourselves. I don't want to sound prideful or anything but we kept thinking about what Jesus said about laying up treasures in heaven and not on earth and how you can't serve both God and material things. So we rearranged our priorities some and Paul helped us find good places to put our money and efforts. I used to be pretty much like most people. I was just concerned with making money for money's sake and doing what I thought was best for ourselves, but now that we've made these commitments I feel like we're not just warming the bench any more, but we're really part of the team."

"You onboard with all this Sharon?"

"Yes, Pastor. I've been involved all the way."

"Wow! Paul, you were right. This is some story."

Paul then spoke for the first time. "Yes, it is and I have watched them through this process. I don't think they're doing it for the recognition or the rewards although the Bible does tell us there are rewards in heaven for good works. They just seem really determined to use God's gifts for his glory."

Stephen nodded his head in approval. "Well, we don't give Christians awards here on earth but if we did I think you guys would be up for the equivalent of an Oscar or a Nobel Prize."

Sharon shook her head from side to side. "No, nothing like that. Now you're just embarrassing us. But I will say that our real reward is how much this has blessed us. Helping in the ways we can has grown our faith. I've always heard people say how much they were blessed by helping others and now I understand that more than I ever did before."

"And we're going to give you a chance to be even more blessed" Stephen said with a somewhat sly grin. "We are starting a class on stewardship. It's not going to be some arm-twisting tactic to get people to dig deeper and give more to the church. But we do want to challenge our members to go beyond what they are currently doing. We want them to see and explore new ways to give their time, energy, talents, and money. Ways that will honor and please God and increase his kingdom here on earth. Some of these will be our own church missions, but some will be worthwhile outside efforts like you have discovered. We want you two to teach that class."

Josh now sat a little straighter. "Whoa! Neither of us has ever even taught Sunday School or anything. We're not teachers."

Paul spoke up again, "And you weren't exceptional givers until you followed God's lead. If you commit to teach, he'll guide you in that too. You know Jesus said that we were to be as smart and shrewd in using money to further the kingdom as other people are in helping themselves. You two have fulfilled that and acted like foxes in the things you've done. You can teach others to do the same."

Stephen then interjected, "It won't be all up to you. Paul has developed curriculum for the course and he'll work with you on it. But we really believe that you two are the real deal and can be both examples and teachers for this class."

As the initial shock wore off, they further discussed the ideas and specifics of the class. Finally Josh looked at Sharon and said, "We believed God before. I guess we should believe him again now and give this a try. What do you think?"

Sharon looked at Paul and Stephen and then at her husband. "Let's do it, big guy!"

And so they did.

# Epilogue

You may have gone to church all of your life or for many years and never heard a sermon based on the Parable of the Unrighteous Steward. It is found in the gospel of Luke 16:1-8. In this parable Jesus tells of an unrighteous steward or manager who has been dishonest with the handling of his master's money. When the master is made aware of this he demands that the steward give an account of his management. The steward, fearing for his livelihood, then goes to three of the master's debtors and makes dishonest arrangements with them to pay a smaller amount than they owe. He does this with the goal of being welcomed into their homes (and probably businesses) when his master fires him. But apparently his master got wind of this and instead of firing the steward, he actually praises his shrewd business dealings. It is clear that the master is just as unethical as the steward.

Jesus is not praising the steward for his actions. He in fact calls him unrighteous. His point is that the sons of the world (unbelievers) are usually shrewder than the sons of light (believers) in how they utilize their money and possessions. We are encouraged to use the blessings that God has given us to further the kingdom. We are challenged to be as shrewd about laying up treasure for the next world as unbelievers are about obtaining treasure in this world. While you may not have heard sermons on this parable, you may well have heard references to two of the verses that Jesus uses to explain the parable to his disciples. In verse 10 he states *"He who is faithful in what is least is faithful also in much; and he who is unjust in what is least is unjust also in much."* Then in verse 13 he says *"No servant can serve two masters, for either he will hate the one and love the other, or else he will be loyal to the one and despise the other. You cannot serve God and mammon."* We are not to live for our possessions but instead we are called to be thankful for them and use them wisely.

This story, Like A Fox, is told as a dichotomy. Part of the story focuses on Marcus who is seen as the unrighteous steward. His story follows that found in Luke 16:1-8. His boss, Antonio, has found out that Marcus has been embezzling money from him and asks for an accounting of the books. Marcus, fearful of losing his position, makes sweetheart deals with three of Antonio's debtors and fixes the books to hide his dishonesty. Antonio however learns of Marcus's dealings and instead of firing him, he praises him and retains him in his current position.

Joshua and Sharon, on the other hand, represent a couple who are striving to be good stewards. They agree that God has richly blessed them, but they have been more interested in using their means for the things of this world than for higher purposes. They determine that if they really believe that everything belongs to God, then they should be generous in using their time, money, possessions and talents to further his kingdom. They are in effect the Sons of Light who have come to understand the importance of investing in the world to come.

While none of us may live up to the standards that Josh and Sharon are setting, the parable should inspire us to examine our stewardship and change our priorities as God leads us to do so.

# ACKNOWLEDGMENTS

Sincere thanks to Doug Walker and to Don and Julie Kawahigashi who have graciously read my stories and helped make sure I didn't go off the rails biblically. Many thanks as always to my wife Priscilla and my daughter Melinda Mabry who read my stories, offered suggestions and did the initial editing. Finally, special thanks to Rachel Bostwick for formatting the book and creating the cover design.

# ABOUT THE AUTHOR

Bobby Watson earned B.A. Degrees in English and History at the University of Arkansas where he also earned an M.A. in History. He is a retired computer software consultant who travelled extensively throughout the USA and began writing memories of his younger years as a hobby, thinking his kids and grandkids might want to read them someday. He then expanded to writing crime novellas and short stories and shared them with friends who encouraged him to publish these stories. He finally decided to take the plunge and the result was his first published book *Twists of Fate,* a collection of five crime stories. A person of faith, Bobby woke up one morning with the idea of writing a book based upon a particular biblical story and the result was *The Testing.* It was well received by his pastor and other friends and led to him writing additional stories based on the parables of Jesus. *The Testing* and these other stories comprise his latest collection titled *Crossroads of Faith.*